All about the
German Shepherd Dog

The 1978 Sieger Canto v. Arminius SchH III. Born 18 August 1972. By Canto v. d. Wienerau SchH II, ex Frigga v. Ecclesia Nova SchH I. Canto is acknowledged as one of the most beautiful dogs ever to gain the title of Sieger. Bred by Herr Hermann Martin, a leading S. V. judge, he is the outcome of many years of patient work and selective breeding. The dog's great harmony of construction, his noble head and faultless backline make him outstanding; and in addition he has rich colouring and great depth of pigmentation. His character, courage and working ability are all of premier excellence and complete the picture of a German Shepherd Dog to stand as a model of the breed. Canto is owned by Herr Johannes Angert.

All about the German Shepherd Dog

MADELEINE PICKUP

PELHAM BOOKS/STEPHEN GREENE PRESS

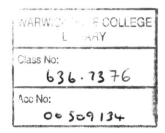
PELHAM BOOKS/STEPHEN GREENE PRESS

Published by the Penguin Group
27 Wrights Lane, London W8 5TZ, England
Viking Penguin Inc., 40 West 23rd Street, New York, New York 10010, USA
The Stephen Greene Press, Inc., 15 Muzzey Street, Lexington, Massachusetts 02173, USA
Penguin Books Australia Ltd, Ringwood, Victoria, Australia
Penguin Books Canada Ltd, 2801 John Street, Markham, Ontario, Canada L3R 1B4
Penguin Books (NZ) Ltd, 182–190 Wairau Road, Auckland 10, New Zealand

Penguin Books Ltd, Registered Offices: Harmondsworth, Middlesex, England

First published 1973.
Second edition 1980. Reprinted 1982, 1984, 1986, 1989

Copyright © Madeleine Pickup 1973, 1980

Made and printed in Great Britain by
Butler & Tanner Ltd, Frome and London

ISBN 0 7207 1219 X

A CIP catalogue record for this book is available from the British Library

Also by Madeleine Pickup
THE GERMAN SHEPHERD DOG (ALSATIAN) OWNER'S ENCYCLOPAEDIA

Contents

List of Illustrations

PICTURE CREDITS

The pictures were taken by Sally Anne Thompson with the exception of
the following which appear by courtesy of those named:
Salassy, Hungary: page 15
British Museum: page 17
Guide Dogs for the Blind Association: page 34
Commissioner of Police of the Metropolis: page 37
Jim Walpole: pages 27, 53, 54, 107
Diane Pearce (*Dog World*): pages 155 *below*, 156 *above*, 157 *left*

Acknowledgements

The majority of the photographs in this book were specially taken by Sally Anne Thompson of Animal Photography. Both author and publisher are grateful to her for the care and trouble she took.

The author also wishes to thank Herr Hermann Martin and Herr Johannes Angert for permission to reproduce the frontispiece picture of Sieger Canto v. Arminius. The photograph is from the archives of the S.V.

Foreword

By Dr Christoph Rummel, President of the *Verein für deutsche Schäferhunde* – the parent club of the breed.

I have read this book, Mrs Pickup's third on the breed, not only with great interest but also with admiration for the expert knowledge she displays of her subject. It is logically arranged to form an exhaustive treatise on the German Shepherd Dog, acceptable to breeder, trainer and pet owner alike.

By her choice of title, *All about the German Shepherd Dog*, she aligns herself with those who give the breed the name which is in common use for it throughout the world, and to which its country of origin rightfully entitles it.* Since it is our aim, in almost every country of the world, to breed this German Shepherd Dog to an agreed standard as a versatile working dog, it is proper, as the book emphasizes, that it should be universally known as the German Shepherd Dog and by no other name.

This book is full of first-rate material, supported always by the author's own experience, on the physical characteristics of the breed and on its up-keep, diet and training. A particular merit of the book is the stress it lays on the rearing of puppies, on making them acceptable members of society and on watching over their health. Alongside the chapters on training are detailed paragraphs on breeding, in which note is taken of the latest research.

I am sure that the chapter describing and explaining not only the system of qualifications and working degrees, but also the very detailed pedigrees issued by the S.V., will be particularly welcome. The German-English glossary will provide invaluable aid to all who are interested in the technical terms of the dog world. Special mention should also be made of the introductory chapter on the origins of the breed, which traces it from the beginning of history through to the founding of the *Verein für deutsche Schäferhunde*, dedicated to producing a dog that should blend physical good looks with courage and a unique quality of versatility.

Mrs Pickup's admirable book will certainly contribute to maintaining the beauty and working qualities that have gained the German Shepherd its outstanding reputation.

*In 1977, under pressure from many of the British national and regional breed clubs, the Kennel Club agreed that the official name of the breed should henceforth be 'German Shepherd Dog (Alsatian)'.

1 Origin and Evolution

It will not be considered a sin of pride, and indeed history will surely confirm my contention that the German Shepherd Dog merits the epithet 'great' in every way. His size and nobility, his many-facetted intelligence, his rapid and ever-increasing popularity as a service dog all over the world and his fantastic records of top breed registrations and show entries are only part of his greatness. His gifted powers of understanding the master he works with, his uncanny foresight and his inviolable character are another part which is only properly appreciated by those who are fortunate and sensible enough to own such a dog. This multi-sided greatness makes him very much a dog apart, and has caused him to suffer jealousy and much bitter and unfair criticism during his rise to the top. However, his qualities are so superior that despite a very bad press, even from his early days in the British Isles, he has now won through and is generally accepted as our No. 1 working dog and first choice for guard and police duties.

His German ancestry has clouded his true origin with obscurity and supposition, and in this book we propose to trace his beginnings back as far as is possible in company with breeds of a similar kind, if only to show that he is essentially a normal animal in his progress and evolution. It is his selective breeding and training by the S.V. (Verein für deutsche Schäferhunde – the parent German breed club) which have made him so outstanding in intelligence and working ability.

All German judges are highly trained in their respective breeds, but to become an S.V. judge takes several years of formative instruction and apprenticeship to an established adjudicator before even a small show can be judged. We will deal with this at length under the proper heading; it is mentioned here only to emphasize the select nature of the German Shepherd Dog.

There is no doubt that the dog which crept into Man's cave possibly 500,000 years ago, also crept into his heart and established that wonderful 'companion to Man' status which was the first link in the chain which has bound human and animal so firmly throughout the ages to their mutual advantage, and which has given us this great dog of service for our own use and enjoyment today. Professor Dr Ludovic von Schulmuth, before his death in 1939, had studied the origins of dogs very thoroughly and had come to the conclusion, with anthropologist friends, that Man and dog appeared at the same time, give or take a few hundred years, in three places, all of them in the Old World. These were:

(a) In central Africa, around Lake Victoria and other lakes in that part of Africa.

(b) In the part of Asia which we now call Turkestan, in the area east of the Caspian Sea, south of the Aral Sea.

(c) In the south-west of the Gobi Desert.

These three 'birth places' gave us the original areas in which *all* the first ancestors of the different types of dogs appeared. As we are writing of the German Shepherd Dog, we need concern ourselves only with the Gobi Desert peoples. The peoples, like all early mankind, lived beside lakes, rivers or marshes (the Gobi Desert was not a desert in those days, a possible 500,000 years ago).

The original dog was wolf-like in type and appearance. So far there has been no actual proof found to tell us if this animal was a 'true' wolf or a very near relation, according to Dr von Schulmuth's theory. These conclusions were arrived at as long ago as 1938 and have been proved correct by more recent finds. Another keen student of canine origins believes that most of the large breeds of dog in Europe are descendants of the jackal (*canis aureus*), and these include the German Shepherd Dog, along with the various types of Wolfhounds and the Great Danes. He considers the Nordic Spitz breeds, which include Elkhounds, Samoyeds and Finnish Spitz (Finsk Spets) are the closest to the wolf (*canis lupus*) in origin, since these dogs in early days hunted in packs over a wide area and lived the true life of these animals, governed by and bound up in their own pack, whilst the 'aureus' breeds are lone hunters with strongly independent characters. I imagine that all of us who have bred and tended German Shepherd Dogs for many years would incline to the theory of the 'aureus' origin, as our dog is certainly an independent thinker, and likes nothing better than to be trained in a job where he can use his initiative and extraordinary reasoning power. On the whole they prefer to be the 'one and only' in their family, and may resent additions to the pack. This adds weight to the argument, since the inborn characteristics of an animal change little over the centuries, despite interference by man in his physical appearance.

An interesting sidelight on the wolf origin is the way the entire character of the breed is changed by cross-breeding with the wolf. This was proved by the Szigethy brothers, who are well known game hunters in Hungary and who made a cross of a European wolf female with a German Shepherd male. Two daughters of this crossing remain in the Szigethy establishment at Gödöllö. In colour they are golden on the legs, throat and muzzle. The ears are also golden, in one case with black edges, and their bodies are a pale grey mixed with some gold. It is curious that either of the Szigethy brothers will enter the wolf's cage

Cross between German Shepherd male and wolf female at the film studio in Gödöllö, Hungary.

and turn their backs on her, even without a stick in their hands, but they *never* go in the wolf/Shepherd Dog cross animals' compound without a stick, nor do they ever turn their backs on them. Their opinion is that the dog blood makes them bold while the wolf blood makes them sly, so that they will never attack from the front. These gentlemen keep a number of wild animals for film work and the original cross of wolf/Shepherd Dog was made because the wolf/dog cross is far easier to train for film work than the pure-bred wolf. However, the shepherd dogs who were filmed attacking in the snow were pure-bred and did some good work.

We know that the small wolf-like animal hung around Man's dwelling from the very beginning. Here he picked up any scraps thrown out by the dwellers, although at first he was shy and afraid of Man. Man was carnivorous and therefore a hunter, but he had only his bare hands and a stout branch or a stone with which to kill his food, and without doubt he noticed that the fast-running wolf-like animal could catch and kill his prey much better than he could himself. So he set himself to trap young animals of this type – which is how in every case Man tames dog. Doubtless, the women brought the small dogs which hung around the dwelling inside, to keep the children quiet and perhaps also to catch vermin.

Later, Man learned to catch wild cattle and sheep, and for these he needed a herding guard dog, which was the second step in the animal's evolution. Then, Man made himself weapons with which he could kill or maim from a distance, and for this sport he needed a dog which hunted by scent, thus he trained the dog to develop his tracking power. Eventually, Man formed villages, and his requirement was a guard dog for his property and for war against invaders of his territory – in short, a war dog. All the original peoples have been shown to have followed this line of development, with the exception of the peoples of Africa.

The peoples of the Gobi Desert area followed in line with the majority. They spread out, however, and their culture varied in different parts of eastern Asia. We are concerned only with those peoples who drifted north, as these were hunters. They moved north over northern Asia into northern Europe, and there found reindeer which they first hunted and afterwards tamed. Their dogs remained true to their original type, that is, either the wolf or the Spitz type, and these dogs were trained and used to move the reindeer herds. The dogs also guarded the herds and their owners' homes.

Slowly, over the years, these peoples drifted into western Europe and swung southwards. Here, in these southern regions, sheep and cattle came into their possession. It is interesting to note that while the dogs remained with their owners in the cold north, they did not alter much in type, only becoming slightly heavier in body and thicker in coat, but as they moved southwards into warmer, sunnier lands they became higher in the leg and lighter in build. There were two reasons for these changes, one being the increase in sunlight, and the other the greater need for speed. For they were now called upon to round up and herd fast-moving sheep and cattle.

Next, these dogs moved down through Holland, Belgium and France into southern Germany. Those that stayed in the north of this latter country remained shorter-legged and heavier in body, more like the original type. The longer-legged type of higher construction passed along the south of Germany and then swung south into Greece, reaching that country about 700 BC. There is proof that the German Shepherd Dog type was well known there by 600 BC, for dogs of this type appear on several different pottery objects. Notable among these is the Corinthian krater dated 600 BC which is now in the Louvre in Paris (see drawing). This shows dogs of the German Shepherd type, coloured either black or creamy white, and sitting, standing or crouching under tables at a banquet. Allowing for the Grecian style of drawing, they give a remarkably clear picture from over 2,000 years ago of the type of dog from which the German Shepherd Dog and his near

German Shepherd Dogs were found in Ancient Greece as is shown on this vase dated 550 BC.

relations sprang. The ears are erect, if somewhat small, while the body is like the German Shepherd in shape, not 'cut up' like the greyhound, which latter is quite common on Greek vases and pottery. German Shepherd Dogs were found in Greece about 500 BC. The picture shows attic black figure on a vase dated 550 BC 'Kylise from Vulci' – The Hunter's Return. On the inside of the cup, a hunter with hound, small prick ears, pointed muzzle (not too pointed), feathered tail and fairly heavy body – neither greyhound nor mastiff type. Professor von Schulmuth always held that the German Shepherd Dog was a *true* Spitz, and that, had the shepherds in Germany not carefully bred the dogs for several hundreds of years, the tails of these dogs would curve over the back, even if they did not curl like the Elkhound's tail. He also asserted that the early dogs used for herding were *never* wolf-coloured, but rather dark in colour so that the shepherd could distinguish his own dog at night should it be engaged in a fight with a wolf, and thus be free to club the lighter-coloured animal and be sure that it was not his dog. The late Dr Erna Mohr, Director of the Hamburg Zoo, wrote about a type of dog which was used to guard the German concentration camps. This dog was originally a native of Bavaria and known for some three hundred years as the South German Shepherd Dog. It was of similar type to our present-day breed, but heavier in build, with a very thick and rather long coat. The distinguishing feature was the colour, which was a pale wolf-grey of the silver shade. The dog was known as the Blau Oberschwaber Wolfhund, and this name was also given to the wolf-grey German Shepherd used in the concentration camps, this colour being preferred as it did not show up at night. Even three hundred years ago this particular strain was noted for its fierce nature.

There is no trace of the German Shepherd Dog type in Spain or Italy before AD 100, although Holland, Belgium, France, Germany and Austria all had this type of dog as early as 400 BC; bones and other evidence have been found as proof of this early existence. The following quotation from an old book will interest (and even amuse) those who are concerned to keep good pigmentation in the breed, as it is indeed required by the Standard:

'GERMAN SHEEPDOG' (AD 1220)

'Have not the white dogs, for their enemies can see them afar at night. Have not the dogs of the colour of the wolf, for how can you strike them in the fight. Have not the pure black dogs, for they are not beheld at darkest night, nor can they hide in the hours of day. Have those dogs which are dark and light, so that they can be seen at night, remain hid by day, and seen when the wolf they fight. Such dogs shall be of good service.'

The Bundeshauptzuchtschau in 1969 was marked by celebrations for the seventieth birthday of the Verein für deutsche Schäferhunde or S.V. (as the parent club is universally known). So our breed, after years, even centuries, of nomadic existence, *always as a working breed*, came to be finally recognized in Germany. There its physical and mental qualities have been jealously guarded during this long period of perfecting the animal, and there one gets startling and immediate proof of the excellent manner in which the S.V. conducts its breeding programme. In the huge classes (sometimes nearly 300 entries in the Open class) the specimens entered are so uniform in construction and character that one is baffled in a first attempt to sort them out.

Although a large number of British breeders visit the Bundes Show each year and some even remain over for the Working Trials, and while the high standard of the breed generally and the few outstanding animals are admired and even coveted by these visitors, it is generally thought that the strict control and guidance exercised by the S.V. would not be acceptable to the breeder in these islands. This is a pity, really. It is the writer's considered opinion that some kind of compromise could be reached, as in Italy and France, where some magnificent dogs have been produced under S.V. guidance accepted on a voluntary basis. In Belgium, too, there are many beautiful and typical dogs bred from German stock; and, of course, these countries are fortunate in having common land frontiers with Germany and, thus, easy access to the top German stud dogs.

It is so easy to be attracted by flashy colouring or over-elegance in this breed, and to lose sight of the especially important construction and piston-like action which are vital in the true working breed. We all admire a good-looking animal. However, he *must* have close couplings, a firm back and muscles, well-knuckled feet and the character and strength to demonstrate beyond all doubt that he is a working dog, and be equipped physically and mentally for each and every of the many tasks allocated to him throughout the world.

In the countries outside the governing influence of the S.V. there has been a definite (perhaps one could say deliberate) tendency over the past two decades to bypass the 'Shepherd type', or to ignore the true working dog in the show ring. This was partly due to the coincidence of a huge increase in show entries (mostly made by newcomers) and the rather 'flashy' eye-catching winners at that time. For, naturally, the novice wishes to win, and feels that he must obtain a dog which resembles the winners at that time, and since he is ignorant of structural and character faults he buys another 'eyecatcher'. So the snowball rolls on until the ring is full of this type, which our newcomer honestly believes to be correct. Also, as first impressions count, when this newcomer becomes a judge (and that is a speedy process these days) he will make his awards to this type, and thus the mischief continues. I often amuse myself by guessing the date of a new judge's first experience of the breed, for almost without exception he will 'put up' the type which was winning at that period.

The reader may be wondering what all this has to do with 'evolution'. It is, however, very much part of the present-day evolution of the breed, and not all of it is good. For we must work constantly to keep the working dog character, the strong nerves and keen senses, the willingness to work coupled with the physical ability to carry this out – in fact, never to allow the 'pretty' or merely eye-catching animal to take over and supersede the German Shepherd Dog proper.

It is not proposed to repeat the chapters on the early days of the breed which have been written by our colleagues the late Mrs T. Gray and the late Mrs N. Elliot. We will touch on the main influences and then our task will be to go forward and keep with the breed as it is today, not always in admiration of the present development, alas! But our aims and objects are directed to helping our modern breeders from where we stand, after forty years of active breeding, many overseas judging appointments as far off as Hawaii, Hong Kong, Canada and the USA, and also several of the African countries, and our frequent pilgrimages to that Mecca of all Shepherd Dog breeders, the annual feast of the S.V., the Bundeshauptzuchtschau – not forgetting the three decades of judging in Great Britain and the wealth of information which comes to us in the compiling of the weekly notes for *Dog World*. None of this not inconsiderable experience makes for a swollen head, let us hasten to say. Rather we feel that the further we travel and the more Shepherd Dogs we see in various countries and climates, the more we are humbled by the greatness of our wonderful breed and by the extraordinary part it plays in service to mankind, and we resolve to play our part in preventing it from becoming a mere status symbol or an over-elegant showdog; in fact anything less than the virile, confident and powerfully-constructed German Shepherd Dog.

Touching on the earliest records of individual animals in the breed, we are told that the No. 1 registration (SZ1) was a dog called Horand von Grafrath (otherwise known as Hektor Linksrhein), bred by Herr Sparwasser, who also owned his litter brother Luchs, whose number was SZ155 – perhaps because he was slow to develop and did not qualify till later in life than his immortal litter brother. With a measurement of 24-24½ inches he was considered large at that time, and we note that the measurement was given as height of back, whereas today we speak of height at shoulder. Captain von Stephanitz describes Horand with great enthusiasm as having 'powerful bones, beautiful lines and a nobly-formed head, clean and sinewy in build, the entire dog one live wire'. But what interests us profoundly is the Master's description of the dog's character: 'This corresponded with his exterior qualities, marvellous in his insinuating fidelity to his master; towards all others the complete indifference of a master mind, with a boundless and irrepressible zest for living. Although untrained as a puppy, nevertheless obedient to the slightest nod when at his master's side; but when left to himself the maddest rascal, the wildest ruffian and an incorrigible provoker of strife. Never idle, always on the go, well disposed to harmless people but no cringer, mad on children and always – in love. What could not have become of such a dog, if we had only had at that time military or police service training? His faults were from a suppressed, or better a superfluity of unemployed energy, for he was in heaven when someone was occupied with him, and he was then the most tractable of dogs.'

We have quoted this description in full, as it clarifies the requirements still enforced by the S.V. examiner for the Körung – that the animal must be inviolable, courageous and intelligent, but also be playful and safe as a children's guard and companion and above all instantly obedient to his owner.

From the foregoing it is easy to see that this is not a dog for everyone who admires his handsome looks and service potential to own, and easier still to see that he is not a dog to keep in large numbers in kennels if his rare intelligence and boundless energy are to be properly used and perpetuated. His enormous reasoning power, his gift of affectionate companionship and his great physical strength must be given an outlet and channelled to useful ends as they were originally intended, or the dog will suffer, and in his unhappiness may become mischievous and even dangerous due to the combined frustrations of lack of exercise, solitary confinement in kennels or the restrictions of city life, which are death to his unique qualities.

We are not going to excuse ourselves for constantly harking back to the character angle throughout this book. It is a matter of major concern to us that this should be properly understood by everyone who proposes to own a German Shepherd Dog, and that all would-be breeders should realize the importance of using animals of sound disposition and of keeping them in such a manner as to preserve these qualities, which spell German Shepherd Dog at his best.

All the history of the breed written in this century points to the truth of its being an amalgamation of several kinds of Shepherd Dogs, and one in which large and small sheep-dogs, long or short-haired animals and even curious colours and white dogs, have gone into the melting pot. In view of these facts it is not surprising that the old adage of it being 'better to own the parent of a Champion than the Champion himself' rings specially true in this breed, since we can never know what the meeting of two prepotent lines carrying, say, long coats or pale colours can give to their progeny. As there are not yet any stud books or reference books going back far enough in this country to warn us sufficiently of these faults, we must do a lot of private research, and investigate all branches of a dog's family before using him in a breeding programme if we are looking for some particular virtue or characteristic.

For breeders in the parent country of our chosen dog it is far easier, as they may seek the advice of the Verein für Deutsche Schäferhunde (S.V.), where a panel of trained judges and Körmeister are available to advise and guide them from records dating back over seventy years. The uniformity of type at their annual Siegerschau speaks for the efficacy of their methods, and when one considers how we, in this country, have to battle on with only our 'horse sense' and the British natural instinct with pedigree stock, we consider that our results, if somewhat less uniform, are nonetheless excellent. This view is often confirmed by visiting S.V. judges. The German Shepherd League and Club of Great Britain issues an excellent handbook every two years in which most Champions appear in photographs. This is a most useful guide for type and markings, although nothing can be learned here of that vital ingredient of a first-class Shepherd Dog, i.e. character. Attendance at the major shows as an observer, especially around the show benches, will give clues concerning the dog's nerves – *not* in the actual show ring, as many extremely shy dogs behave quietly here when they are carefully trained and conditioned to ring atmosphere. We consider it essential to see a dog outside the show ring before assessing its true character, particularly as any real character tests are not permitted in our show rings in Great Britain.

Remembering that the true basis for the breed's development at its beginning was the selection of dogs with skills in herding and cattle guarding, and considering its enormous popularity as a show dog, due to its outstanding beauty, it is really surprising that it has not suffered more in temperament and loss of its original characteristics during the post-World War II period, with its great increase in numbers as a guard dog, a family pet, or even a status symbol in frequently inexperienced hands. Indeed it is a tribute to the early breeders and those who fashioned the German Shepherd character that the dog has come through so many changes, and even assaults on his disposition, and is still the Number One service and utility dog throughout the world, and that largely by these means he continues to attract (and hold) more and more devotees. A few figures are of interest here, and will help the reader to assess the importance of the breed in many fields. In 1982 the membership of the Verein für Deutsche Schäferhunde (S.V.) was around the 145,000 mark, and that year their great show, the Siegerhauptzuchtschau, attracted 1,500 entries, with the Open class accounting for just over 300 dogs.

In Great Britain, which can justifiably be considered the breed's second home, the registrations rank among the highest at the Kennel Club with some 12,000 to 14,000 dogs annually. At the shows, too, the German Shepherd generally tops the entry with classes of thirty to forty exhibits at Championship Shows. It could fairly be said that our judges require as much stamina as the handlers of this fast-gaiting animal, since an entry of up to 200 dogs is a long day's work.

In Switzerland the German Shepherd comes into his own as a worker. The army uses the breed extensively for messenger and liaison work, and when one considers the mountains and deep valleys, which would take a man many hours of difficult and even dangerous climbing to cross, it is easy to see how useful a trustworthy, well-trained dog can be in communications, as he can traverse the roughest terrain at speed in all weathers. The Swiss police value our breed highly, too. In the towns there is approximately one dog to every three officers, and one dog for each man on the beat in rural areas.

These are a few statistics taken at random to illustrate the gigantic scope and range of the breed's activities throughout many countries.

There are other aspects of importance which will appear in the chapters ahead. We never cease to be thrilled at the accounts of rescue work in avalanches, and other brave acts carried out by the breed, and we propose to include some outstanding ones in this book, not forgetting the wonderful work done by the Guide Dogs for the Blind, which touches everyone's heart. So it may be seen how the German Shepherd Dog has remained through the ages of development and change, both mentally and physically, a first-class – even unsurpassed – working dog. It is this part of him which has won through adverse publicity and jealous attacks on his trustworthiness, to bring him universal acclaim for his outstanding beauty and his service to Mankind.

2 The Construction

The first impression of a good specimen of the breed is of a firmly-knit animal with strong muscles, dry bone structure, a noble head proudly carried and an overall harmony of outline with substance and strength. An alert, eager outlook is desired, also a handsome appearance, but not overdone or 'pretty' enough to mask the working quality of the dog, nor yet a soft or cloddy look which is completely alien to the breed. Sex character is also of great importance, and there should be a marked difference between dog and bitch, the bone structure of the male being distinctly heavier, without being massive or clumsy, whilst the female has a dainty appearance yet shows no sign of weakness or lack of working ability.

We will go over the dog from head to tail, and discuss the structure and points throughout. The head should be of proportion to suit the size and type of the dog. Although an over-heavy or coarse headpiece is to be faulted in a male animal, it is to be preferred to one of 'bitchy' appearance lacking the noble masculine characteristics. The bitch is more refined, with the same nobility, and any coarseness is a serious fault here. A clean-cut look, with only a slight arching of the forehead, no roundness of skull or abrupt stop. The muzzle is powerful and wedge-shaped (but *not* collie-like), and above all the lips must be firm, and close tightly without flews. The ears, which form an essential part of the general appearance, are of medium size, broad-based and preferably fairly thick and firm in texture. Thin-textured ears, which are not rigid during movement, are faulty as are over-large ears, which spoil the clean look of the head, or ears too small in size, which lend a 'foxy' appearance which is untypical. The ear carriage is also important; ears should be placed fairly high on the skull, open to the front and well-pricked, as the animal uses them to indicate his alertness. A lack of perfection of ear carriage should not, however, be heavily penalised provided that the texture is firm and they are both completely erect.

The eyes are of great importance, since they reflect the dog's disposition more than any other single feature. Almond-shaped and never bulging or prominent, they are slightly oblique in setting and of medium size. Colour is very much a subject of controversy. They should be a soft, dark brown with a direct forward look and full of expression, keen and intelligent, but showing complete composure.

A well set-on head with soft, dark eyes and erect ears.

The colour is permitted to match the surrounding fur, but must never be yellow. A wild expression or a rolling eye is a sign of weak nerves, while a very dark eye, lacking the fire of intelligence, denotes a dull or dim-witted animal useless for work.

The teeth really require a whole chapter to themselves, since they are vital to the dog's ability to perform many of his tasks. Forty-two in number, with twenty in the upper jaw and twenty-two in the lower, they are powerful in development and close in a scissor bite – with each tooth in line with its fellow in the other jaw and the top ones just resting on the lower ones and slightly overlapping. This scissor bite is immensely strong and enables the dog to grip far better than one where the teeth meet edge to edge; the wear is less, too. A mouth where the lower teeth fail to meet and close with the outer surface to the inner surface of the upper teeth is 'overshot' – a serious fault. The opposite, where the under jaw is overlong and the teeth too far forward to engage with those in the upper jaw is deemed 'undershot' – an even more serious defect.

Returning to the number of teeth, the extra two in the lower jaw are after-molars or grinding teeth, while the pre-molars are eight in number, two on either side of the upper and lower jaws, and it is these teeth which cause anxiety in many breeders' hearts, as they are not unexceptionally short of the full number, and this is a serious fault as it is strongly hereditary. In Germany a dog lacking more than one of the small pre-molars – Nos. 1 or 2 – cannot be given a Class I certificate at the Breed Survey. Dogs which lack not more than two of the small pre-molars (i.e. Nos. 1 or 2), and also those with slightly undershot (i.e. level) bites, are admitted to Class II only. If an animal has more than three of the small pre-molars (Nos. 1 and 2) or more than two of pre-molars No. 3, or one of pre-molar No. 4 missing, or if the bite is over or undershot, then the progeny is not eligible for entry in the studbook of the S.V.

It will thus be seen that a correct mouth is of great importance, and since faulty dentition is definitely transmitted it must be given careful consideration in the breeding programme. The full dentition, the clean and closely fitting lips and the true scissor bite are an essential part of the Shepherd's equipment in dealing with a criminal, rescuing people from snow drifts and other work where a strong, tenacious grip is required. It is not a fad of the show ring, but one of the dog's foremost assets in his work. It should be mentioned, so that undue anxiety is not caused to the novice, that ear carriage and the bite change considerably during the first six months, even the first year. The lower jaw may grow faster than the upper, or vice versa, and the missing pre-molar may suddenly appear – we have even heard of one which came through the gum at two years, although this is exceptional. With ears it is another

Two dogs showing sex character. On the left the feminine head and expression of a young bitch, on the right the strong masculine head and outlook of a mature dog.

story. They can continue to strengthen and gain firmness up to eighteen months, and there is no doubt that the link between ear carriage and teething is considerable; even humans suffer earache when they have a bad tooth, so it is not to be wondered at that ears drop or falter when the puppy is cutting teeth.

The neck has a big part to play in the general appearance. It is not always taken into full consideration when assessing an animal, despite its influence on both outline and elegance. Of medium length, it should be both powerful and well muscled without loose folds of skin or dewlap. It should be long enough to give the forward look of a German Shepherd (in show reports 'reaching' or 'good reach of neck' means just this) and held level with the top of the withers at normal times, but raised up to give the alert appearance when excited or interested. It is also a sensitive point of control when the collar or slip-chain is worn. An ugly and unpleasant handling trick has been used in the ring of recent years, where the slip-chain is pulled up tightly just behind the ear to give the head a raised and alert carriage. It also prevents a nervous or restless animal from moving into a normal stance, and can even deafen the dog if pulled really tight against the ears. From the show angle it quite spoils the natural outline, straightens the shoulder slope and gives a giraffe-like appearance quite untypical of the breed.

Apart from this, it is also a cruel and painful method of asserting one's mastery over a dog, and has been much criticized by visiting judges to the UK. Above all, the neck must fit on to the body very smoothly and be free of any throatiness, which coarsens the appearance considerably. A good ruff is very pleasing as the colouring of the hair here is usually prettily shaded, especially in sables.

Now we come to the withers, sometimes referred to in show reports as 'the top line', and it is at this 'point of scapula' (shoulder blade) that we assess a dog's height. Also from here comes much of the dignified appearance we all strive for in our dogs – rather like a man with a well-carved pair of shoulders. At the withers the slope down of backline to the croup begins and, taken in relationship to the overall length of the dog, this is comparatively short. (The total length of the dog is measured from the point of the prosternum to the tail root.) The back is strong and firm, showing no alteration in harmony of line when moving, and should be quite straight. The loin, where the body and hind-quarters are coupled, should be broad with an elastic firmness (not 'stuffy') and never too long or the back will be weak. It should, above all, blend smoothly into the back so that one is not conscious of its separate function.

The finish of a good, firm backline lies in a well-shaped and correctly sloping croup, with a good tail set on properly. The croup should have sufficient length (short croups give a 'clubbed' and clumsy appearance to the rear end and restrict the hind-quarter action) and should slope gently and gradually down. If it is too level it will restrict the length of hind-quarter thrust in action by preventing the reach under the body.

The tail is one of the glories of this beautiful dog. It should be well furnished with bushy fur and set smoothly into the croup fairly low down. A high-set tail will spoil the outline and give a square appearance to the croup. In length, the tail should reach the hock joint at the very least, an inch or two longer is more normal. It should hang with a *slight* sickle curve when at rest, and rise slightly away and outwards from the hocks when in movement. When the dog is excited it may be carried level with but not above the backline. A longish tail which is carried to one side in action is not a serious fault, even if it is not harmonious, but bent tails and the corkscrew variety are to be penalised as ugly faults, while 'clubbed' tails with thickened ends due to ankylosis (fusion of the vertebrae) are serious defects.

The body of the German Shepherd Dog is not easy to describe. It should have an impressive depth without any suggestion of clumsiness, a solid build with ample heart-room, and yet be shapely and clean in line as befits a working breed. The length of the body should somewhat exceed the height at the shoulder. This proportion excludes a dog of 'square' appearance, also one which is too high on the leg. The chest is defined as the prosternum, which is the foremost point of the forechest, and this should be well filled-out and carried right down between the forelegs without hollows or 'shellyness'. The chest proper is part of the body where the depth should be of ample capacity for the heart and lungs, and with a forward development carried beyond the shoulders when studied from the side view. The ribs are deep and well-sprung, although not barrel-shaped, but more spring is allowed in the female, particularly if she has had a litter. Too flat or 'slab-sided' ribs are faulty. The depth should carry down to the breastbone, which is level with the elbow. Properly shaped ribs are important to movement, as the elbows must not be impeded by any excess springing when they move back in action, since this throws them outwards and destroys the smooth reach of the front legs. A rib cage carried well back gives the desired close 'couplings' when the loin and flank are comparatively short.

The abdomen or underline can mar the clean appearance if it is paunchy and soft, but it should not be 'tucked up in loin', as this gives a greyhound-like look. This is one point in the dog's anatomy where feeding and exercise are clearly reflected – sloppy food gives a sloppy underline, lack of exercise gives lack of firmness in the abdominal muscles. Naturally, a matron just off her litter is allowed some latitude in this respect. In the chapter concerning maternity we will discuss this more fully.

We want to mention bone formation now and in particular that of the legs, for the leg bone is most easily noticed and a Shepherd Dog requires strong, straight front legs and clean hock bones at the rear end. The quality of the bone is important. It has an oval, almost flat appearance and is very strong and firm; roundness and a 'spongy' texture are most untypical and should be faulted. Correct bone is often referred to as 'ivory' (by the Germans as 'dry'), and the clean, hard look reminds one indeed of ivory. The sloping joint at the lower part of the front leg is called the pastern and this plays a great part in the movement of the dog. It must have a noticeable slope (not steep, like a terrier) and be both firm and elastic, as it is the shock absorber which controls the smoothness of the outreaching front stride of the Shepherd Dog. It must be strong, and never overlong or exaggerated in the angle, or the foot will react in much the same way as the human one which flops on a weak ankle instead of being firm and steady at both walking and trotting speeds.

After the legs we come to the feet, which are of paramount importance to a working dog (or person, for that matter!). Ideally, these are fairly short with the toes compactly held and the pads deep, thick and hard to enable the dog to grip well. The claws should be short and strong, and preferably dark-coloured, although light-coloured claws are not really a fault – this is more a question of prejudice among breeders (and judges). The rounded, short 'cat foot' is not desirable, while thin pads, weak and spreading toes and long, 'hare' feet are serious faults. The structure of the foot is a complex part of the dog, and if it is naturally good it will always return to proper form through exercise, even after long periods of illness or inactivity. A poorly constructed foot can be greatly helped and improved by climbing up steep and stony banks or running on a shingle beach, but it will lack the strength and beauty of a normal one. Poorly muscled feet on overlong and weak pasterns, which fling about as the dog moves towards one have been a serious fault in the ring in recent years and one which should be heavily penalised if newcomers are to be educated as to what kind of feet are required by the Standard and, more important, for the work of our breed.

We want next to consider the front and hind assembly, together with the much over-used – and even more misunderstood – term 'angulation'. Exaggeration in angles produces weakness and renders the dog unfit for his proper mission; it gives an over-elegant and therefore an un-Shepherdlike appearance. Lack of angulation gives a stiff and stilted action and takes away the quality of the animal which may, however, be strong and completely fit for any job of work normally done by our breed, although his turn of speed when herding may be somewhat less than his correctly angled brother.

When we look at the front assembly, we notice particularly the shoulder placement, for the shoulder is the lever of the front limbs and governs the length and soundness of the front stride. Many novices mistake a well-developed forechest for a good shoulder angle – the two are entirely separate, and a dog may well have one without the other. An over-developed forechest gives a 'pouter pigeon' appearance and may well fool the inexperienced eye into thinking that the dog possesses a good shoulder; in fact, the upper arm is too long, which causes the chest to protrude. The upper arm is the bone leading from the point of the shoulder joint up to the point of the scapula (or shoulder blade) at the withers, the rounded upper end of which should be in vertical line above the elbow. The ideal angle of the shoulder is in the region of 90 degrees, in fact a right-angle. This figure gives the necessary free forward reach, as it allows the leg to travel well back under the body without destroying the firm line of the withers. To enable this assembly to fulfil its proper function firm ligamentation is essential, and many well-placed shoulders are faulty in action through loose muscles. Older animals, particularly bitches, sometimes develop heavy muscles or fleshiness on the exterior of the shoulder line, and this can restrict the freedom of the forward reach. This is often referred to as 'loading' in the shoulder. Excessive climbing or jumping before the dog has completed its growth is said to cause this loading or excess of muscular development. A steep shoulder will cause the dog to lift the front legs too high as he strives to co-ordinate with the hind-quarter thrust. This co-ordination is not possible without correct shoulder angulation, which opens fully in action allowing a free and sweeping forward stride. Another point which must be watched in the front assembly is the elbow, which should not turn either in or out, for these faults could cause a variation in the sequence of steps. Finally, the forelegs should be straight when viewed from all angles.

The hind-quarters are the subject of much controversy among breeders and judges. The structure is more easily discerned than that of the forequarters, and there are many fierce arguments over the degree of angulation required (or desirable). One thing is certain, however, and that is that overangulation (i.e. exaggeration of the angles) is both undesirable and untypical of a working breed. It renders the dog unfit for long hours of untiring gaiting and – even from a merely aesthetic point of view – it spoils the balance of a properly constructed animal. Here again, a well-constructed rear end is insufficient in itself; it must have firm muscles and not be over fleshy, which gives a clumsy finish to the animal.

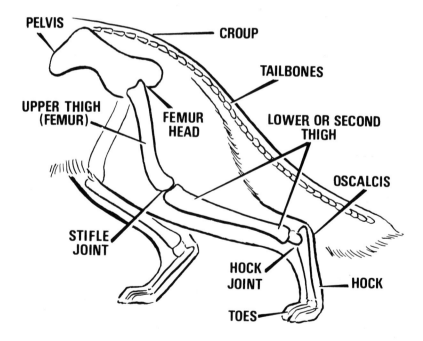

The angle of the thigh bone should parallel that of the shoulder blade, while the stifle bone parallels the upper arm, in the ideal construction of a set of sharp angles formed by the relation of one bone to another in the hind-quarters. The thigh should be broad but not fleshy, and both thigh and stifle should have strong well-developed muscles and be of proportionate length, making practically a right-angle. The lower part of the hind leg, from the hock joint (or tarsus) to the foot, is commonly referred to as the hock, although its correct name is the metacarpus. This should be clean in bone, short and powerful, with the joint sharply defined. The stance should be firm and straight and not 'cow-hocked'. However, real cow hocks are more noticeable in movement than in stance, as some well-angulated animals tend to stand slightly cow-hocked when relaxed, and this should not be faulted if it is not also apparent when the dog is moving away.

Colour assumes great importance in the eyes of the novice, but counts for comparatively little in the estimation of an experienced breeder or judge. *Pigmentation* is often confused with colour; this former, however, is of great importance since lack of it gives 'washy' colouring and pale noses and pads. To in-breed on poorly pigmented animals will assuredly give white puppies, which may be very attractive in the nest but which are not allowed by the breed Standard (they are indeed barred from the German Breed Survey) and render the dog unsuitable for guard work. They often grow up into ugly specimens with pink noses and eye-rims, and so should hold no place in thinking breeders' plans. It is quite natural that the newcomer's eye should be taken by flashy colouring, and many excellent dogs do carry bright golden tan or red tan and black colour which attracts attention. However, this same lovely colour covers many a fault, and the learner's eye must go well beyond it when choosing a dog. A dark mask is most desirable, with the eye as dark as possible or at least as dark as the surrounding fur, and with dark rims.

The coat of the German Shepherd is not only of great beauty but also one of its great assets when working outside. The double coat, with its strong guard hairs, shining and waterproof, over a thick, downy undercoat, is excellent equipment for a working dog; the body warmth is trapped between the two coats, and the animal remains warm and dry through quite severe weather. The undercoat is soft and woolly, lying close to the skin, while the top coat, also of a close growth, should be strong in texture with the hairs lying close and straight, which makes them weatherproof. A slight waviness in the top coat is permitted, also a harsh or wiry texture as long as it is not curly. Very short coats or long silky ones are serious faults from the breeder's angle. If the long coat is open-textured (falling into partings) the animal will not be suitable for work outside, since this type of coat is not weatherproof. In Germany, such a coat precludes the animal from being passed for breeding.

The normal coat is shortest over the head, including the ear-furnishings, and over the front of the legs, the feet and the toes. It is longer on the backs of both fore and hind legs, stopping at the pasterns and the hocks respectively. The hair thickens over the neck to form an attractive ruff, and is softer and somewhat longer along the belly. The hind-quarters have a dense and slightly longer trousering, which gives good protection to the organs when the dog is working outside. The tail is covered by a thick undercoat and harsher 'guard' hairs overlying it as on the body. These are, however, softer, longer and often paler in colour on the underside of the tail. When the dog has to sleep outside in cold weather, he buries his foreface in the effective protection of his thick, warm tail covering. It is considered that long, soft or open coats are not adequately waterproof, afford less than the protection required for the working dog and could diminish his stamina and resistance. Animals with such coats should not be used for breeding. It is often noted that a dog with a 'Collie-type' coat tends to have a narrow chest and a long, straight foreface which increases the Collie appearance. Many of these long-coated specimens have lovely dispositions, too, and though precluded from breeding they can nonetheless make useful companions of handsome appearance.

3 The World's Leading Dog in Service to Mankind

Stories of the German Shepherd's role as the No. 1 service dog, in dozens of varying tasks, make fascinating reading for those already 'hooked' on the breed, and bring satisfaction to new or would-be owners.

There is no doubt that our breed's popularity as a working dog has caused jealousy among other breeds, and we rather think that some of the stories circulating about its 'treachery' are from the same source. The newcomer may well ask why the German Shepherd is so superior in the working or training field? We will endeavour to enlighten the enquirer in this chapter from what we know of our dogs' achievements

Perhaps the most touching aspect of the breed's work. A guide dog takes her owner to his job.

to date. Fresh tasks are being found for him all the time, tasks he will perform to astonish and gratify his trainers and confound the few (getting fewer all the time) who do not join in singing his praises. We will go so far as to say that when there is a job for a dog (and some which could even be considered beyond him) the German Shepherd will do it as well as any other working breed and far better than the majority. There are many reasons why our dog is a suitable, even superior, choice for his ever-growing variety of tasks. Physically, he is ideal; large enough to be imposing, yet not clumsy or slow in action. Naturally endowed with strong muscles, he can trot tirelessly for hours (when properly conditioned by freedom and exercise) and he is an excellent jumper and scaler of fences and walls. His lovely double-textured coat gives him perfect protection for long hours of work in bad weather conditions and in extreme climates. His stamina and resistance are first-class. A merciless tracker of criminals and contraband, he is also a guardian whose keen vigilance is often mistaken for fierceness. Such a quality is not a natural part of our dog and in any case is not required for his guarding duties where his courage and determination are his normal 'weapons' and make him the police dog par excellence. His long history as a sheep-herding dog has endowed him with a deep-rooted concern for small animals and invariably for children, with whom he displays his protective qualities at their best. We will include a few stories of incidents which illustrate these points later in this chapter.

THE POLICE DOG

As far as can be ascertained, the honour of introducing the forerunner of the modern police dog on the continent of Europe belongs to the late Dr Gerland of Hildesheim in Germany, early in 1896. It is also generally understood that the city of Ghent in Belgium was the first to establish a regular training establishment for police dogs for local use, at about the same time. These are most likely to have been Malinois (Belgian Sheep Dogs) or even Tervuren, which has a distinct resemblance to the German Shepherd of the long-coated variety. The earliest record of civilian Police Dog Trials were of those held by our parent club, the S.V., in 1903, with a programme of tracking and man work. In England today, at least six training societies hold P.D. Trials each year, and in the majority of these the winners are German Shepherds trained by members of the police forces. Although civilian owners train very keenly and many of their dogs excel at man work, there is naturally not the same scope for such a highly-trained animal in everyday civilian life as there is in the forces, where the dog is on duty constantly with his handler. We have no hesitation, rather the greatest pride, in saying that the wonderful training given at the Metropolitan Police Dogs Establishment is acknowledged by visiting police officers from all over the world. Their most advanced and effective methods are admired and copied with great success, and trainee handlers of every kind can be seen undergoing instruction at the 'school' at Keston.

To return to the dog himself. Only a very few animals are acceptable to the police, who require not only first-class nerves, but unusual intelligence, outstanding stamina and condition with courage, determination and a good disposition as well! Quite a list of qualities to be found in a single dog. Yet to most of us they spell 'German Shepherd Dog', and account for our deep feeling for our beloved breed. The selection of a puppy for police work is not easy; in fact it is as difficult as picking out a future champion for the show ring, and with possibly as many pitfalls and disappointments. Everyone has a pet theory in the sorting out of a litter or in testing a more mature puppy – one officer always put his cap on the ground to see if the puppy is interested in a strange object or has the wrong kind of reaction, or, just as bad, shows indifference. Others will make teasing play with a piece of cloth, to see if the puppy will 'go in' and sieze it, which they usually enjoy doing. The real aim is, of course, to see if they are determined enough to hold on. About twelve weeks is the best age to run the rule over a promising 'cadet', and, given normal luck plus a suitable and sympathetic handler, the results reveal a high percentage of successes.

It is unfortunate that the lay public are of the opinion that the police dog is necessarily a ferocious animal which is trained to attack and is therefore potentially dangerous outside his own field of work. Just as a police officer is first and foremost a member of the community and secondly a 'copper' and tough when required, so like master, like dog. I wish that these uninformed critics could see some of our police dogs which live happily as normal family pets, when off duty, in the homes of their handlers, where they are highly esteemed members of the family. We know of one policeman's wife who gets out of bed if there is a night call for the handler in bleak weather, and gives the dog warm milk with a spoonful of brandy so that he does not take cold – the husband just gets a 'cuppa'. But that dog has an impressive list of arrests to his credit. Demonstrations are given, mostly at summer events such as fetes and agricultural shows. In this way we hope always to improve the image of our dogs doing their most important job, i.e. assisting our hard-pressed police forces in their difficult task of maintaining order in a world of disorder.

The training of police dogs is basically the same in all forces, with some adjustments for the kind of territory where they are to be used eventually. We are not at liberty to disclose these methods, but we must emphasize, once again for the beginners, that not one cruel approach is allowed in the dog's education, and no tricks of any kind. It is largely a question, as the song has it, of 'doing what comes naturally'.

In other words, developing the dog's normal instincts to such a peak of perfection that he guards, tracks, defends, jumps and scales, uses his nose, eyes and ears and his in-born reasoning power, just as naturally as he once did in his wild state many hundreds of years ago – only this time in co-operation with his much-loved handler.

Top dog Vico 'searching and bay-ing' after finding a criminal.

Corporal punishment is absolutely forbidden. A dog is always corrected by a scolding voice and an attitude of displeasure on the part of the handler; and we all know that they hate being 'in the dog-house' just as much as we do ourselves! But we have had repeated evidence from the many overseas police and training experts who have visited our police centres for instruction that we lead the world in dog training, and several have been incredulous at the wonderful results shown at the end of the carefully-planned and scientific basic course of only six weeks duration.

THE DRUG-DETECTION DOG
If this is one of the most recent operational fields for a dog it is certainly also one of the most important. Since drugtaking, and the smuggling, distribution and sale of drugs are high on the list of crimes

in many of our larger cities and towns, and since those engaged in this unsavoury business are keenly sought by the authorities, the role of the dog has assumed great importance. The majority of drug-detection dogs at present are Labradors; the breed lends itself extremely well to nosework and is assiduous in searching. It is also not so immediately identified with the police, so that it does not arouse alarm or suspicion when out on the street with its handler or even when making a few private investigations, and this is a big advantage in such work. It does not enjoy the imposing appearance of the German Shepherd, but it is easily trained, quick to learn, and has a solidity of build which is very useful in bringing down a man in the chase. The most recent set of figures known to the public shows over five hundred arrests made in one year by the drug-detecting dogs. Many other useful jobs are done by the dogs in this branch, such as dealing with persons suspected of possessing drugs, where the only evidence is provided by the dogs' special skill in detection.

The Prison Dog

During the past decade the use of dogs as extra security-guards in prisons, particularly at night, has been developing. This is largely due to the enquiry held under the late Earl Mountbatten, which made, among other recommendations, one which advised the use of trained dogs as part of the security force. Prison security patrol work is somewhat monotonous, and the company of an alert and well-trained dog is valued by those carrying out this exacting task. The animals selected for this work do not have to undergo quite the same rigorous training required for the full-time police dog. Their work is less varied, but they must be under full control in all eventualities, and fully proof in the exercise of food refusal, the search for persons or property and the essential attack or 'stand off'.

The presence of a dog patrol at a working party when the prisoners, sometimes twenty-five in number, are often quite free during the working period, is increasingly valued by the officers in charge of these men. It must be a fact that the knowledge that the dog could follow them instantly and 'hold' until his handler arrived, or even be on the trail within minutes if given a clue, is bound to act as a deterrent to would-be escapers. Prison dogs are trained by special instructors at the police dog training establishments such as Keston and Durham, and represent one of the largest forces of working dogs in the country today.

Parks Dogs

Most of the London boroughs employ a handler and dog to patrol their parks and open spaces, as do the municipal councils in many other cities and towns throughout the British Isles. The primary object is to protect women and children from being molested in the recreation centres, to safeguard their property and amenities and to prevent undesirable characters from sojourning in bushes and shelters. The dogs are also useful for finding lost children and property. The park attendant himself is vulnerable in these days of hooliganism, but with a trained, trusty dog at his side he is unlikely to suffer personal attack. These dogs mostly live in their handler's home, where they are family pets. They are not 'multi-handled'.

ROAD SAFETY

Another excellent job done by the breed is the teaching of road safety drill to schoolchildren. A specially trained handler (again employed by the borough council) goes, with his dog, a mock zebra crossing and other apparatus to simulate roadside conditions, to schools and recreation centres. Here the dog gives a demonstration of kerb drill, moving his head from left to right and retreating to the kerb if a vehicle approaches suddenly, with various other demonstrations of road safety conduct, all of which impresses the youngsters far more than any human display!

DOGS WITH THE ARMED FORCES

Our dogs have an endless variety of tasks here, and many have been 'decorated' for bravery. In times of war they perform highly skilled and dangerous missions, as well as saving many lives by giving warning of enemy presence, detecting explosives, and by their special work with the Red Cross. As sentries and guard dogs for airfields, supply dumps and vital installations they are unsurpassed, and, as with the police force, their watchfulness and presence are of real comfort to the men on lonely duty in all weathers. Their work as mine detectors has been especially valuable although, alas, many have lost their lives at this dangerous task, a fact regretted by all, even if it meant that many human lives were thus preserved. When in South Africa, I saw a 'tickey' – an old threepenny piece, and very small indeed – buried in some rough ground. A handler and his dog arrived by car some time later, the dog was put on the search, and within six minutes came back, carrying the coin rather gingerly in his mouth. It is not suggested that the dog should discover a mine; the exercise is to prove that a dog can scent metal, quite odourless to us, when so trained to do it. The breed's fantastic ability to identify almost any object by scent has been exploited in numerous ways, and we will deal with them in their relationship to the several branches of work described.

We do not know anything (perhaps fortunately) of warfare in the future, or whether our dogs could be of the same wonderful service to our defence forces as in the past, but in mentioning some of the excellent work done in recent wars, we pay our humble tribute to the many who died a hero's death.

In all the armed forces, guard work is routine to both man and dog. Much of the time it is tedious, monotonous and (seemingly) unrewarding. Here our dog does great service as an alert companion to the on-duty man. He is also a splendid saver of manpower, since in protecting large areas where supplies and stores are kept and in patrolling the vast perimeters of airfields and long stretches of coastline, one sentry with one dog are said to replace seven men. At the many military tattoos, and particularly at the Royal Tournament which is one of the highlights of the London summer season, our breed puts on a spectacular display, usually with the Royal Air Force, who train their dogs for all kinds of stunts to maintain their keenness and obviate boredom on lonely stations. We saw a splendid display in Salisbury, Rhodesia, where the dogs appeared unaffected by the heat and, as always when working with informed handlers, were willing, happy participants in the exercises. There is a good spirit of competition among the handlers and much pride in their cheerful 'partners' in duty, something which impresses and delights the onlooker.

The dogs which worked so nobly with the Civil Defence during World War II must also have their mention here, and their achievements could fill many pages. Many of the stories are well known to those who lived through that period in our large cities – a time of anxiety and often terror – but we will give a few details to indicate yet one more facet of the range and ability of our dog at work. One of our senior breeders, the late Mrs M. B. Griffin, M.B.E.,of 'Crumstone' fame, worked with her dogs at the Ministry of Aircraft Production School. Her two 'stars', who did much to assist in the training of the several thousand dogs which went through the School, were named Irma and Storm. Storm was a powerful, black dog, bred by Mrs Griffin out of her sheep-herding bitch Crumstone Echo, and had qualified both C.D.Ex and U.D.Ex. This splendid dog worked through some of the worst raids on London, during which he located more than eighty casualties in the bomb debris. Irma was Storm's daughter and was awarded the canine 'V.C.' – The Dicken Medal for Gallantry. She saved a total of seventeen lives from those buried or injured in the raids, and was credited with finding at least 200 buried casualties. Another famous 'Dog of War' was Jet of Iada, also an all-black like Storm. He was bred by Mrs Babcock Cleaver and was worked by Corporal Wardle, a brilliant handler, who controlled Jet perfectly and under whose guidance this dog, also, gained the Dicken Medal for Gallantry.

THE HERDING DOG

In Great Britain, the German Shepherd Dog is perhaps less used as a sheep or cattle-herding dog than he is in Europe generally. This may be because there are already several excellent working breeds native to these islands, and which have a warm place in our farmers' hearts because of their centuries of reliable work. This is something we readily understand, and do applaud. However, it is a great pity that our dog does not have more consideration for this work, which is, after all, that for which he was originally destined, as his title indicates. Imagine how trustworthy the guardian of pedigree cattle and sheep must be, likewise those who are required to watch over valuable bloodstock without disturbing or exciting these highly-strung animals! The choice of a German Shepherd is a natural one, and, with his instinct to protect anything small or weak, he is reliable with all young stock, too.

Here at Druidswood where our pride in our great family of top-ranking police dogs is immense, we are also happy at the number of useful 'farm workers' which are bred down from our bloodlines, and it would appear that their intelligence applies equally to both tasks. Two widely different accounts of the affectionate concern our line has in this respect are given here. One of our Roon z.d. Sieben Faulen daughters – and a tough little girl, too – served her 'time' with the Metropolitan Police, and gave them several litters of useful stock. When her retirement came, she went to a family who owned Toy Poodles, which Nadya quickly adopted and treated as puppies – much to the indignation of one of them, who was twelve-years-old and was absolutely furious at being pinned down by a large, gentle paw while he was thoroughly 'topped and tailed' by an equally large and wet tongue! Then our current 'Head Boy', a hefty 90-pounder, just will not keep out of the run where we keep our newly-weaned litters. 'Poor wee things', he seems to say, and over the wire he leaps to wash faces, play silly games, and finally herd them into a corner until they fall asleep, when he will lie in front of them in proper sheep-dog fashion. The surprising thing is that the dam of the puppies is also running free, but makes no attempt to interfere with the self-appointed baby sitter and shows no anxiety over her babies.

We have plenty of dogs in Great Britain which carry strong herding blood, and, as my stories indicate, the ability and instinct to herd and care for stock is latent in many of our dogs – in particular through the descendants of the great sire of the 1930s and 1940s, Voss v. Bern and his granddaughter Maureen of Brittas, owned by Mrs J. Beck. In fact, all Brittas stock seems to have herding ability, and this is fostered and made use of by their breeder, Mrs Barrington, who gives all her dogs the opportunity of developing this side of their character on her extensive property in Eire.

Lapislazuli of
Druidswood   C.D.
ex, herding dog owned
and trained by
Mrs D. Tustian.

This uses of a dog with herding instincts are many on farms and where breeding stock requires protection. A large number of turkey farmers keep a couple of dogs as guardians of their feathered flocks. We have had worried turkey breeders telephone, towards the Christmas season, to ask where they can obtain, or even hire, a guard dog to keep the thieves away. Turkeys are notoriously difficult to herd, but I have seen a single German Shepherd bring in 1,000 birds at bed-time with no more than a few indignant squawks from the turkeys – truly a praiseworthy enterprise. Another family owns a house cow, which grazes in a paddock some distance from the cow byre. At milking time, the dog is sent to fetch the cow which wears a short rope halter, and by this the dog leads it expertly to the byre, giving a few sharp barks to advise the farmer that the cow is now ready to be milked.

On the Continent, our breed is very much the working dog. If their owners are perhaps less sentimental about their dogs, at least the dogs have good lives with freedom and plenty of scope for their great intelligence – the life our dogs would all prefer if offered the choice, I am sure. In Germany, the dog still has its true place as a first-rate sheep dog, and can be seen at work all over the country. These dogs are lean and hard in condition, and run tirelessly all day in every kind of weather. Since there are few, if any, hedges or fences to separate pasture from the growing crops, the shepherd uses his dogs, which run up and down the whole day keeping a sort of 'living fence' around the flock, while maintaining a vigilant look-out for any sheep that steps out of place towards the succulent crops so temptingly near. In hilly or mountainous districts the sheep are driven away from the pastures which are required for hay, and spend several weeks high above the farm grazing on the plants or herbs that they especially enjoy. The shepherd spends this lonely period with his flock, and often uses his dog to carry messages down to the farm in the valley below and to return with provisions and other commodities strapped to his back.

At the great annual Hauptzuchtschau in Germany, the HGH (Herdengebrauchshund) Special class attracts an enormous crowd of onlookers. Curiously (or is it?), the number of bitches entered is almost double the dog entry, and it is also interesting to note that most of the animals entered are by top 'V' or 'V.A.' sires. Notable among these are Argus v. Adught SchH III, Vasco v. Kirschental H.G.H., Lasso di Val Sole SchH III, Vax v.d. Wienerau. Another good producer is Jalk v. Fohlenbrunnen, SchH III. We mention these names as pointers to any reader wishing to trace the lines through which the good herding blood flows, and also to show that the winning dogs at the Sieger event are not merely beautiful, but also full of the working ability which is a large part of our breed's attraction all over the world.

4 A Little About Training

A reader who is a potential buyer may well ask, after the preceding chapter, whether he or she will ever learn the skills necessary for training such wonderful animals. Never forget that all of these great performances began with a normal puppy, predisposed to mischief, a slip chain and a lead, a pair of firm and gentle hands, and an endless supply of patience. In other words, 'Big trees from little acorns grow'. So if you feel that you would enjoy the task, start with the elementary obedience training. Should you decide that the advanced work is not for you, you will at least have the reward of an obedient dog, under proper control, which can go anywhere and be accepted as a decent, responsible member of society, besides being a good advertisement for the breed and even a feather in your own cap!

The earliest lesson for most puppies is to be house clean, and this we will deal with in the chapter on rearing. We do feel that apart from this most necessary training, and perhaps training the youngster to sleep on his own bed rather than yours (or your favourite chair) and to chew bones but not shoes etc., serious training should not be started until he is about four months of age. The more advanced training should not be attempted till he is one year old.

The first step is to establish your dog/master relationship, and during this period you will both learn much which will be of use in the teaching and acceptance of instruction which follows later. One must play with a puppy – they are usually lonely after leaving their litter-mates and kennel companions. Spoil him a little at first with an odd tit-bit of cheese or a digestive biscuit, or a cube of well-boiled liver hidden in the pocket or the hand to make a game for him. Tickle his chest and roll him over, gently of course. In this manner he will learn to turn to you for pleasant reasons, and this gives him confidence. If possible, do give him his food yourself, and let him out in the morning and put him to bed last thing with his 'goody' and a special fussing, so that his day begins and ends with you, his master.

While the puppy is learning to look up to you, watch carefully for his early reactions to strange sights and sounds, as these may usefully guide you in his adult training period. We have come to the positive conclusion that every dog, even the bravest and toughest, is afraid of something. If we can discover what this is in early days, we can do a lot towards minimizing the fear, even perhaps overcoming it, by recognizing the dog's reaction and sympathizing with his anxiety. German Shepherd Dogs invariably want to please their owners, and will even do things they dislike doing if their attachment to the trainer is based on affection and confidence.

One example of this was a dog, of otherwise perfect temperament, in our own kennel who was terrified of anything dead. In fact, he would not pass in front of a butcher's shop, or even a fishmonger's, but would drag me across the road to the opposite pavement. This fear was so strong that he could smell or sense dead animals anywhere. I used to visit a friend who lived at the end of a road which began with a very high wall, and this dog would cringe and flatten himself when we entered the road by car. I mentioned this to my friend one day, and she said that the high wall surrounded the local abattoir! While we were never able to conquer this fear completely, we did overcome it to a great extent by teasing him into playing with a dead rabbit in its skin, but this took hours to accomplish and several sessions without any headway at all. I always felt that had I discovered this fear in his puppyhood, it might have been completely cured.

It is, I believe, universally recognized that a dog's eyesight is not nearly so keen as his hearing or sense of smell (the Greyhound and Whippet excepted). This may be the cause of some sensitivity in the reaction of our breed to sudden and unfamiliar noises or to strangers or objects of unusual shape – their ears and noses respond, but their sight is not so keenly developed, and this confuses them until they are gently persuaded to approach the fresh object or strange person and sniff, and they are near enough to get it into proper focus.

For this reason, and we may mention it often since it cannot be over-emphasized, no training at all should be given and as few changes as possible made in the routine and surroundings of a young puppy which goes to its new home at nine to ten weeks old. It can be utterly confused if commands are issued by its new owner and a kaleidoscope of fresh faces, voices and hands come into its new existence. Remember that a sensitive puppy is better training material than the over-playful extrovert, which has one strong and simple idea – just to get its own way, and at your expense. The puppy must first of all be given every opportunity to grow accustomed to the scent of the new owner, remembering that it is the sense of smell that connects us with our dog, and that it is through this avenue that the dog learns complete affection for his master and confidence in his owner/trainer. Von Stephanitz wrote that 'Trust is a sine qua non and obedience is the foundation of all training.' Both go hand in hand, and both are inseparable. So, let him sniff your hand frequently, touch his head, caress him, groom him and examine him, all with your own hands. Do not forget the hand should be used only for caressing and guiding and never, *never* for punishing him, which can be effected with a few taps of a rolled-up newspaper – the noise being the greatest deterrent. Punish only in extreme cases; your dog may be disobedient, but he is not a criminal, so correction may be given frequently but punishment rarely, if at all. The lesson here may be taken from the manner in which a bitch deals with a refractory puppy, she may well growl, or even shake it by the loose skin round the neck, but she never bites or harms it in any way during correction.

Most Shepherd Dogs are natural jumpers and enjoy showing off their prowess.

We have the greatest admiration for our training clubs, and are also most interested in the Working Trials, but as these words are more likely to be read by a novice or pet owner, and less by experienced trainers, here is a paragraph especially for the former. There are plenty of well-behaved, obedient dogs which have never been to a training society, but owe their good conduct to the understanding and sympathy which exists between them and their owners. Their good behaviour stems from a desire to please a beloved master or mistress – and nothing is more compelling to a German Shepherd Dog. Your warm praise is their reward, and your affectionate consideration maintains their standard of obedience. *Of course* he is naughty and destructive as a small puppy, and *of course* he will challenge you with his own will in adolescence. Yet, his delight in your praise when he understands the lessons taught with patience and consistence will give you a yearling who enjoys his responsibility as a proper member of society, and who will go through life with the hallmark of an intelligent German Shepherd Dog in his unswerving devotion.

A well-known Continental trainer once said that to be a good trainer one had to put oneself in the dog's skin! In other words, one had to look at training from the dog's angle. This advice is particularly good when one takes over the new puppy in his strange, fresh surroundings. Imagine his loneliness, the chill of the solitary bed after snuggling up with his litter-mates, the boredom of being without playmates and the food which is less attractive without the spice of competition in the feeding bowl. Be with him as much as possible, teach him that even if he is left alone you will return, give him some old shoes and a bone to play with, and even hand-feed him a bit until he is accustomed to eating alone. But – this isn't part of training? Indeed it is, and vitally important – a getting-to-know-you which will establish the sure basis of all training, that is, the complete trust and the mutual affection which are the first steps to all those glittering honours which await the well-handled and correctly trained animal.

Having established your good relationship with your puppy, the next step is to teach him the two lessons which are essential for his safety, to walk quietly on the lead and to come when called. We like a light slip-chain on our youngsters. It should be three or four inches longer than the girth of the neck to be comfortable and effective in use, since the noise of the chain being drawn up acts as a signal to attract the wearer's attention. In these days of rising costs, one does not wish to buy a new slip-chain every week to keep pace with the puppy's rapid growth. We usually buy one several inches too long, and fasten the surplus links together in the centre with one of those plastic-wire bag fasteners from supermarket packages, to make a sort of pendant in the middle so that it does not interfere with the slip movement, and then release a link or two as growth requires.

Let your puppy wear his slip-chain collar for a few minutes each day at first, so that he is familiar with the feel of it and will not associate it directly with the restriction of the lead. *Never* allow him to wear the slip-chain, now or later, when unattended or if he wanders. If the chain should catch on a nail or similar object he can easily hang himself in his attempts to get free, and we know of at least one sad case where this happened.

Now your puppy (shall we call him Bero?) is used to wearing his slip-chain, so he should go outside with you to a quiet place and be placed in the sitting position at your left side. Next clip on the lead, put your hand under his chin so that he is looking at you and say in a clear tone 'Bero, heel!', while you step forward giving a gentle tug on the lead, which is held in your right hand – with the fingers *through* the loop, please – and controlled about half-way down by the left hand. You will probably get one of two results from your command; either Bero will sit tight and give you a dirty look, or he will leap in the air and give an imitation of a newly-caught fish! You will also be getting a lesson, one of patience and calmness, with your sense of humour always at the ready to save you from the exasperation of an oft-repeated command which may take some time to bring results. Don't confuse him by talking to him or using any other words than the command, just bring him quietly back to your left side, make a fuss of him, repeat the order and try again and again, praising him warmly and treating the matter lightly to give the puppy the impression that training is fun for you both. You can keep a tasty tit-bit in your left hand for the first few lessons, so that Bero is interested in following you for the reward you may eventually give him. A bit of cheese or baked liver wrapped in a small plastic bag is most convenient, so that at the end of the session he will sit attentively while you unwrap the goody. Above all, school yourself not to feel discouraged if you do not obtain results immediately; some puppies take to the lead as a duck to water, while others are headstrong and independent and come to terms with these first restrictions very slowly. However, ours is the working breed par excellence, and it is rare to find a puppy that does not respond to a patient but decisive approach.

These early lessons must be kept short – about ten minutes each day will suffice – and after a week or ten days you should have Bero under control on his lead. When he will follow you and seems to accept that he is attached to you by his lead, then walk on, turning gradually to the left in a large circle so that he comes against your leg as you turn. This will accustom him to move close to you and enable you to check him from forging ahead by moving left, so that your leg obstructs him as you give a short jerk on the lead with the order 'Bero, heel!'. If his training has to take place indoors, you may find it useful to practise in a corridor or passageway so that the puppy is forced to walk between you and the wall on your left. This will curb him if he prefers his freedom – and he probably does! You can, of course, equally use a wall out-of-doors.

Praise must be generous and convincing. A few tit-bits will help if given when he reacts to the command, or for any improvement shown. In any case, you must keep the session going until there is some show of understanding, so that it ends pleasantly for you both, with the ring of your praises in his ears. Otherwise if you stop on a correction you will have an unwilling pupil. Training is repetition and more repetition, and is only leavened by the dog's delight in pleasing you and receiving your praise, and by your own pleasure in seeing his understanding of your commands and his response to your methods. You should allow him a few minutes of freedom between the exercises, so that he comes back fresh to the next attempt; and you can also throw off your own tension meanwhile. Don't forget that your joy in walking out with a dog at your side who does not exhaust your strength by pulling ahead depends on your success here.

Obeying your call 'Bero, come!' is the next lesson, and one essential for his safety. This exercise will be the first proof of the link of affection and respect forged between yourself and your puppy, and which should have been built up during the earlier lead training. Don't call the dog repeatedly or unnecessarily, or he will become bored and indifferent. In a clear, breezy tone call 'Bero, come!'. Clap your hands or slap your leg, even whistle to attract his attention, but remain perfectly still yourself. When he comes to you, take hold of him and welcome him warmly, endeavouring to 'catch his eye' and make him look up to you. It is better to do this exercise when the dog is hungry towards his meal time, then you can reward him with a goody and he will be eager to return to you. Take care to call him in a bright, encouraging tone of voice, for if you shout or sound angry you will only succeed in scaring him; or even if he does come in he will look cowed, with ears pinned back, which is a poor reflection on yourself.

Another method successfully used by many trainers employs a 20-foot long, light check-cord (a nylon one is excellent). With this cord fastened to his slip-chain, the puppy wanders around, and when he is busy investigating some object or scent, you call him as previously indicated and at the same time give a light tug on the lead. If he fails to respond to the recall and to the tit-bit you offer temptingly, he must be gently 'reeled in' and praised and given his goody. For although you may feel it is undeserved, it is essential to associate his return, aided or unaided, with reward. These rewards of food will be largely discontinued when good habits are established, although nobody can have

Use of the tracking line to teach the reluctant dog to come smartly to recall.

failed to notice that circus dogs, and performing dogs in stage acts, are always given a small goody when they have completed their work.

In teaching the recall, it is totally wrong to go after the puppy. *You* must stand firm, and *he* must come to you. If you run after him even once, he will gather that this is some sort of game, and one which he is equipped to play far better than yourself. In fact, he will see a chance to win. So stand quite still, and if his response when free is half-hearted, then turn your back on him and walk slowly away, when he is most likely to become curious and will come up with you. Then you must give him warm praise as usual, for any step towards understanding is an achievement you share with your dog, and he may well give you a lick on the hand and a tail-wag to show you his pleasure in being reunited with you, which is your praise from him. When these two lessons have been mastered – and you may well spend three to four weeks of short daily sessions – do not neglect to repeat them frequently. Ten minutes daily is perhaps the minimum period, although it will suffice if the puppy has made normal progress, and will keep him keen and responsive by the regularity of the exercises. Short though they may be, these will form a better basis for advanced training than longer, tiring and certainly more boring sessions at the weekends only. Above all, watch yourself during this early training. Never attempt instruction when you are under stress or upset, for your mood will quickly be transmitted to the dog. You cannot reasonably expect to control your dog if you are not in control of yourself.

Training is usually associated with outdoors, but as we live (and many others do, too) in an uncertain climate, we want to give a few exercises in obedience which can usefully occupy days when the weather is unsuitable for taking the puppy outside. All puppies have a natural inclination to carry things about in their jaws. New owners are always lamenting the loss of shoes, gloves, handbags and other suitable (in Bero's estimation) articles for a puppy to play with, or even just for the fun of collecting and the satisfaction of possessing these playthings in his bed. As we have already mentioned, we must watch the trend of the puppy's behaviour, and learn how to develop his good instincts as well as correct his bad ones. So we use this passion for carrying objects to teach Bero to fetch. In other words, he will learn the important task of retrieving from his puppy games. As his mouth may well be tender from his teething at this time, we like to start by using a medium sized wash leather. This is light and easy, even for the most sensitive mouth, and has the advantage of being washable after use.

Have Bero by your left side, and shake the leather to gain his attention and interest. Then throw it a few feet in front of him and clearly give him the chosen command which you will always use in future training, coupling it with his name thus: 'Bero, carry!' or 'Bero, fetch!', spoken in a coaxing tone. Bero may be unimpressed or even puzzled. So, if he makes no sign of understanding, lead him gently towards the skin, pick it up, and shake it teasingly until he seizes it, which is usually almost at once. Now return to the first position with Bero at your left side, settle him down, and then throw the wash leather again and give the clear command simultaneously. He will most probably make a quick dash to retrieve and shake the leather, although you may have to exercise your patience several times before he grasps the idea. As he picks up the wash leather be ready with your praise, 'Clever boy, Bero!', using a delighted tone so that he senses your pleasure. It is unwise to force the leather between the puppy's jaws for fear of hurting him, as this could make him reluctant or even unwilling to retrieve or carry in future. Just playfully shake the wash leather and tease him into grabbing it, and then release your hold as you praise him; do *not* allow it to become a tug-of-war between you.

After you have succeeded in getting him to take hold of the wash leather, or to fetch it a few times, you can progress to his next lesson. Walk away, slapping your left leg and encouraging him with your voice to follow you. After a few steps, stop and bend down to open the puppy's jaws carefully with your left hand and extract the leather with your right. Bero may have to be manoeuvred into a corner first, so that he cannot follow his normal inclination to rush off with the toy. When you have him under control, be very firm with the quiet order 'Drop, Bero!' as you take the leather from him. Now praise him, patting his head or tickling his chest so that he does not get flustered or excited. Be very careful of the manner in which you praise your puppy. Keep your voice low and warm in tone, and while the words you may use (usually a sort of baby talk!) are not so important, the actual key words are vitally so. Thus, *good* or *clever* are connected with praise, and *bad* and *no* are for scolding and link up with correction.

Another lesson which can usefully be taught now is to sit and remain sitting until told he is free. This is not perhaps the easiest exercise to teach, as it involves going against the puppy's natural instinct (which you have been encouraging until now) to follow you and be near you. At this age (four to five months) Bero could develop an interest in the surrounding world, even to the extent of attempting to visit the neighbours or wandering to the garden gate. If he is taught to sit, it will curb his instinct to roam and help him to appreciate that his duty is to be with you always or, at the least, encourage him to keep his attention on you, anticipating a call to join you for some pleasant reason, even just a pat and a 'Good boy!' which means so much to him.

This exercise is made easier if you begin when Bero is hungry – shortly before dinner-time is best of all. Have some small goody (we use cubes of baked liver, clean and tasty) in your right hand, hold it a couple of feet above his head, to gain his attention and as you do this give the command 'Bero, sit!', using your left hand to give firm but gentle pressure on his hind-quarters so that he sits. Then, as he reaches the sitting position, quietly praise him and let him take the tit-bit from your right hand. Don't on any account allow him to have his reward if he jumps up to claim it; push him down again, and then he may have it if he sits quietly. The gesture of the raised hand and the pressure of the left on his rear end will soon connect in his mind, so that eventually he will go into the sitting position when you raise your hand with the command 'Bero, sit!', and you will reward him with praise long after you have dispensed with the tit-bit, of course.

When you are satisfied that young Bero is sitting quickly and willingly, you can extend this lesson to the 'sit – stay!'. This exercise is particularly useful if the dog lives indoors, since it teaches him confidence in your certain return to him when he has to be left in a room alone, or when you cannot take him out with you. It could save a lot of paint from being scratched off doors and the chaos one finds in a room where an unhappy, lonely puppy has been seeking an exit to follow the beloved owner. This may be raising queries in the minds of experienced trainers who use the 'down – stay' position when leaving their dogs for a long time. However, Bero is very young and must be left occasionally; we want him to be assured of our return to him and he cannot learn the advanced exercises yet.

This 'sit – stay' is a 'must' if you intend to show your puppy when he must be benched and, unless you have a supply of 'baby-sitters', he will sometimes have to remain quietly alone on his bench while you are occupied with other matters. So you will find that this is something really worthwhile teaching him, even if it takes considerable time and patience. For, we repeat, Bero's natural impulse is to get up and follow you. It may not sink in for several sessions that *you* want him to stay while *he* wants to come with you; he may feel at first that it is not fair play, so make the lessons short and be lavish with rewards.

You may like to start the session outside, in which case find a quiet place (always better for the initial lesson in any exercise) and put him on his lead – the same drill if the lesson is started indoors. Get him to sit facing you and hold the lead in your left hand, meanwhile raising the right hand which Bero will associate with the signal, and try to catch his eye by moving your forefinger and talking quietly to him. Then, putting all your willpower into the command, say 'Bero, stay!' in a low, firm voice, endeavouring to fix him with your eye to make him remain in the sitting position while you, also, stand quite still. After a couple of attempts, and if you are both patient *and* determined, Bero will sit and watch you attentively as if wondering what happens next! This is your cue to move backwards a couple of steps away from him, warning him to 'Stay!' You may now progressively lengthen the distance between yourself and the puppy; and eventually you will be able to go outside the door and find Bero patiently sitting awaiting your return. This may take two or even three weeks to accomplish, but do remember to return Bero firmly to the original sitting position should he move at any time, and NEVER make the mistake of calling him to *you*. The objective is for him to remain there until you return to *him*, when you will quietly praise him so that he is not roused to leap up and greet you.

When you have mastered this last exercise together, you have the basis of a combination of more interesting exercises using all three in a variety of lessons, all of which will take lots of time and tax your patience to the full. You can teach Bero to sit and stay by your left side while you throw the wash leather ahead; teach him to return to the sitting position with the skin in his jaws; and he can be taught to sit at your left side when you stop during his lead training – a quick slide of your left hand over his hind-quarters will drop him into the sitting position.

The future success of your training programme hangs on your progress with these early lessons. Both Bero and yourself are adjusting to the business on hand – he has to learn to be attentive and obedient, you have to remember to be both patient and fair. Children and dogs have a lot in common, and as it is said that a child's character is formed in the first seven years, so with a dog's short life the first six months

Left: 'I'm Tawny and six months old. While Sid, our trainer, watches, Mum is teaching me to jump – only 15 inches high to start with, of course.'

Right: 'Cousin Lex is two years old. He is showing me how easy it really is.'

are the important formative period. Be firm, fair and consistent. Don't be indulgent and then expect Bero to understand when you are harsh in an attempt to regain the ground lost during your indulgence. Always remember that dogs are extremely practical and will think out quick and easy methods to obtain results with the least bother to themselves. In fact, they are experts in finding short cuts to success! And don't become a victim of canine blackmail – the barking and whining until they get a tit-bit from your meal table, the refusal to eat unless hand-fed and fussed over. If you intend to train, even if only for a good companion, you must steel yourself against these early attempts your dog will make to train *you* to do as *he* wishes. You must show Bero quite clearly that you are the trainer, and that your will is stronger than his at all times. So he will realize that by his obedience and by doing things your way he will get praise and reward and a comfortable way of life; but that if he is inattentive and disobedient he will invariably earn reprimands and correction. The German Shepherd's great intelligence will not take long to work out that it is easier and more rewarding to be obedient, but the matter is really dependent on you. Your keenness is transmitted to your dog, your understanding will generate his devotion, and your long-suffering patience, your iron will and complete self-control only equalled by your sense of humour will make you a suitable instructor to this great breed and bring you satisfaction and pleasure beyond that of the ordinary dog owner. We wish you all possible luck.

Left: 'Lex says, "When you are two this is how high you can go." '

Right: 'Then Lex shows off and goes Wheeee over an 11 ft 6 in. long jump. He just loves doing it.'

5 About Purchasing a Puppy

If the foregoing chapters have moved the novice reader into a desire to own one of these truly remarkable dogs, we would like to go over the many factors which govern the choice and purchase of a puppy. It must first of all be appreciated that the puppy will spend all its life with you and that you will have it for its allotted span – say eight to ten years. So it is extremely important that the matter of buying a puppy is given very careful thought.

We will start with the personal aspect, suggesting that you look ahead to the time when this small, enchanting bundle of fur (along with Chow Chows, ours are the prettiest puppies to be seen) is a large, active dog, brimming over with energy and wanting daily a good deal of exercise and care. Please do not think of taking on a German Shepherd without deep personal cross-examination, nor without consultation with your family, who will surely be involved in its welfare and whole existence. The best home is one where everyone wants to have the puppy, so that it is welcomed and received into the fold and assured of its correct diet and attention to its needs. Puppies mean lots of work so if you are not energetic, or at least an all-weather walker, but prefer to spend your leisure before the television, don't buy a German Shepherd as a companion. Although he may lie uncomplaining beside your viewing chair, this should only be after his exercise or training period and not because it's 'too hot' or 'too cold' to walk, or raining, or some such excuse for not taking the youngster for what is to him the event of the day, as well as an essential matter for his health and condition.

Then there is the question of space and accommodation. The little fellow may well curl up on a small mat in your kitchen during his early puppyhood, but when he is over six months old and weighs about 60 lb he will need a large, comfortable bed where he can stretch out and not be under everyone's feet. If you are thinking of having him sleep out in a kennel, he must never be put there after spending the evening by the fireside, or he will get both chills and rheumatism. The kennel must be large enough for his comfort and completely damp-proof and draught-free and furnished with a large bed. There is also the question of fencing to be considered. A small wooden fence may be adequate for a young puppy, but if you have neighbours who also have dogs, you will most likely require 6 ft chain link fencing to help you preserve the peace!

We would also like you to think about his cost of living. The price of dog food keeps pace with that of our own, and this is not a dog which can be maintained on table scraps and a few dog biscuits. While they are not dainty feeders, German Shepherds need plenty of plain, good quality food, mostly meat, or they do not develop the bone and muscle required in a working breed, and they quickly become victims to skin troubles if unsuitably fed. You can enquire at the pet shops for the current price of horseflesh, and your butcher will tell you if he can supply ox cheek or ox heart at reasonable prices – not mince, which is mostly oddments and fat, and in any event not suitable for our breed, as I shall explain in the chapter about diet. At the time of writing, we are paying 40p per pound for top-quality horsemeat; the same meat cost under 5p thirty years ago, so it is with some feeling that we advise you to go into the cost of maintaining your future pet.

There are all the usual 'ifs' and 'buts' attached to buying any kind of puppy to be contemplated. If the lady of the house is very house-proud and values her immaculate polished floors, then four-footed friends are going to create problems unless you have a dog room or enclosure attached to the house and intend that young Bero should always remain outside. The car gets hairs on the seats, and your clothes also suffer (those that you can afford, after paying for all that meat!). Don't overlook the passionate interest dogs have in gardens – they dig energetically (holes!), they transplant rose bushes and flowers to unexpected parts of the garden, while lawns are the most comfortable places for them to 'spend their money'. Finally, a dog cannot be left in the house like a piece of furniture while you go off for a weekend or on holiday. He must either go with you, which will restrict your movements, or he must be sent to a boarding kennel – and the good ones are naturally not cheap.

We hope that the foregoing paragraph does not sound depressing. It is not meant in that light. We only wish that we could get the message over to the many otherwise charming people who thoughtlessly buy a German Shepherd and then find it is a misfit. We work quite closely with the local Dog Rescue Society, besides running a 'service after sales' on our own puppies, and could easily fill a chapter with the reasons people give for wanting to sell them or give them away (and even take them to be put down), many of which are the outcome of ignoring the 'ifs and buts'. For those whose lives are incomplete without a canine companion, these lines have no meaning. We just feel so badly for any puppy, and particularly for one of our own sensitive breed, if it does not have the affection and attention necessary to make it comfortable and happy, and if, as is quite frequently the case, it is passed on to another home when its puppy sins or the expense turn its original owners against it.

If you are satisfied that you really want a puppy of this breed and that none of these horrid warnings apply in your case, then we will make a few suggestions as to how best to go about your purchase. One method, which is especially suited to anyone with a show puppy in mind, is to buy the weekly dog papers, and find some shows which are convenient for you to visit. Go along and look for the type of animal you fancy, and then watch those that head the classes – not at just one show, but several, if possible. Enquire from the breeders of the ones you favour if they have any promising stock available; or, if there is a particular dog which takes your eye, ask if he has sired a good litter (or litters) which you could go to see, and make an appointment. Be sure to have a few chats with the exhibitors (everyone likes to talk about their dogs!), and you should be able to work out something constructive after a few show attendances.

Should your heart be set on a puppy for training, it would be better to find out the name of your local training club and its venue – the Citizens' Advice Bureau can help you here. Then go along to a training session to enquire if anyone knows of some puppies from a strain with working ability. There are some strains which excel in obedience, others in working trials, and then again some (yes, even in our breed!) which are not gifted for work. For a beginner to find a puppy of the correct temperament and potential for training is to get off to a flying start in what is surely a very competitive field. Here again, as with a show puppy, it is worthwhile, even necessary, to take time over your enquiries and make sure you have full information about the puppy's ancestors before buying, and not to take home the first cuddly ball of fur that catches your eye or captures your heart!

If a good-looking companion is your goal, you are the easiest person to satisfy, and when this kind of buyer comes to our kennel I am envious, as he only has to find the puppy he likes or which likes him. So the lovely one whose mouth is not quite right or who has a heavy coat may find a loving home with this person, who is only looking for a charming character of good type and never has to worry about the many details which concern the show-goer. While we would all like to breed (and own!) the perfect dog, we are afraid that this animal does not come in every litter, but in a good, reliable strain there are always handsome animals whose faults are often minor ones, and only discernable by critical and expert judges. Provided that the greatest essentials, i.e. sound nerves and a kind disposition, are possessed by the puppy, then he can be a very useful companion and guardian, an excellent working animal, and give pleasure to his family and owner. One has to remember that plain-looking humans are frequently the most charming!

The next big question is which sex is the most suitable. Again, one must consider the requirements of the buyer. For the future breeder, or anyone starting in the show ring, a bitch is the certain choice. If she has been carefully chosen from good bloodlines and still does not make the heights in the show ring, she can yet make a good brood bitch, and carefully mated she may give you an improvement on herself in her litter. The mothers of many of our best show animals have been quite plain-looking, but their breeding must have been good and they often did not pass on their faults, which is one of the things a breeder can find out only by experiment. Many beautiful champions have left nothing behind them in the ring, just as numerous ordinary ones have produced a wealth of winners. This is one good reason for starting with a bitch, since a dog, unless he is outstanding and a big winner in the show ring, is unlikely to be used at stud except by a few people nearby. Campaigning a stud dog is also a very expensive business, requiring both experience and time, so it is hardly for our beginner.

For a companion, particularly if there are small children around, a bitch would be the natural choice, since her inborn concern for all young things will cause her to be patient and tolerant with youngsters who do not always realize that puppies need rest, and that they resent being teased or pulled about when they want to sleep. Children are often even cruel to one another, and unless they are well drilled and supervized, their small hands can inflict pain on a sensitive, growing animal whose sense of fair play will be outraged by rough or inconsiderate treatment. In an ideal situation the child and the dog are taught mutual respect and consideration – we will leave you to guess which one learns faster! Once a few rules have been established, and provided always that you have chosen a puppy from a reliable line with sound nerves, you will have the family guardian par excellence, a sort of super nanny, in fact!

If you live in a community, you may have some thoughts about the drawbacks of the bitch's bi-annual periods of heat. A well-fenced, dogproof garden is a 'must' if you intend to keep the bitch at home during her seasons. There are a number of effective dog-deterrents on the market, and one of these deodorant aerosols, used on her hind-quarters and along gates or doorways where her admirers may sniff, is helpful. She may also be dosed with some full-strength chlorophyll tablets (we find human ones superior to the animal variety). However, none of these products, useful as they are, will prevent a bitch's normal mating desires, and she will need close supervision at these times, since even the most obedient and docile ones will endeavour to escape for illicit union with, perhaps, a most unsuitable partner.

If you are able to keep your bitch at home at these times, so much the better, but she will suffer badly from the lack of her normal exercise, and complete confinement is really cruel when she is accustomed to her freedom and walks. You can get over this to a certain degree by taking her in the car to somewhere far enough from home so that the interested dogs cannot follow the scent back to your door, but she must be kept on the lead and carefully watched during her outings. She will be clever enough to take advantage of any lapse in restraint on your part, so do not give her any opportunity to use her wiles. If you lack the facilities required or are too busy to give 24 hours supervision for the heat period of between 21 and 28 days duration, you may prefer to make enquiries about a clean and well-conducted boarding kennel where she can go for her bi-annual 'holidays'. Your bitch's breeder may help you here; some breeding kennels take boarders themselves, which may be the ideal solution. Certainly they can recommend a reliable establishment where our breed is accepted and properly cared for.

Lastly, if you do not intend to use your bitch for breeding, you can have her spayed when she has matured or is well over her growing period – after her second heat is about the right time. If done before then it interferes with her normal development and could affect her other glands and their functions. To those unfamiliar with this operation, let me say that it is a simple one, very much a routine one in a veterinary surgeon's life, and consists of removing the ovaries. Afterwards, she will not come into heat or be attractive to dogs, or even have a desire to mate. Usually, she can be removed to her home for nursing as soon as she is out of the anaesthetic, and the discomfort lasts only for about 48 hours. A young, healthy animal is soon back on her feet and her food, and, when the stitches have been removed, ten to twelve days later, she can resume her normal life. Only in rare cases is her personality affected, and if she gets over-weight it is more likely to be caused by her being indulged at meal times, or having insufficient exercise, than by the operation. Male dogs are devoted and loyal in much the same way as bitches. However, they have the masculine failing, with a possible few exceptions, of being interested in flirtation the year round, and may be tempted to leave home to pursue the 'Beckoning Beauty'. This is the chief reason why bitches are chosen, invariably, for guide dogs for the blind, and is worthy of your consideration when making your choice of the new pet.

Perhaps you are having thoughts about the colour of your puppy. This is, of course, a highly personal matter. In Great Britain our show rings have been filled of recent years with black and tans or golden tans of various depths of colour, with quite a lot of the undesirable (by the Standard) colour paling. We have already mentioned that colour must not be confused with pigmentation, despite their close connection. Whatever colour your chosen puppy may be, he *must* have a dark nose, and dark toenails are preferable. Puppies change colour quite a lot with maturity and usually tend to become lighter, so it is wise to take one with deep, rich pigmentation and as much black as possible. A sable puppy should have black tips to the hair and preferably a dark mask. Dark eyes are better in any colour, although the Standard allows that they may be the colour of the surrounding fur. Perhaps the expression is the best guide. Some very dark eyes have a blank, expressionless stare; the Shepherd Dog should have a warm, kindly look which kindles when he is alert or roused to defence, and becomes very keen.

If you are really serious about a puppy for future show purposes, it will pay you to have a look at both parents before buying. A prepotent parent can stamp its type on a small puppy, but with maturity some of the undesirable or unattractive faults from the other parent can develop and give you an unpleasant surprise. When you have made up your mind on all these points you may find yourself at the kennel, full of enthusiasm and eager to select a future champion! May we suggest a few things to look for which will guide your selection of a sound one, even if it never wins a prize? (If it were easy to pick a winner we should all have rows of champions.) Still, we can note soundness and temperament even at this early stage. Ask the breeder if you may handle the puppies, taking care to be very gentle. We have often noticed that puppies seem to select their owners, so be on your guard in case the attractive little creature that seems to be pleading to go home with you is not, in fact, the one you would prefer. Note the way that the puppies move, their action should be vigorous and even. All puppies naturally have a loose, rolling action when very small, but their limbs should be straight and strong with firm bone, and the action light and swift, with no tendency to stumble or drag the hind feet. Put your hand in between the front legs to feel if the prosternum is established and the chest is not hollow. Check the mouth very carefully. Most puppies hate having the jaws opened, but you will want to see if the 'bite' is fairly even, although mouths *can* have an overshot or undershot bite at this stage, which will usually recover with maturity. If you are in doubt, ask to see the parents' mouths.

Without giving offence to the breeder or attendant, you can check a few facts concerning a puppy's health while handling him. He should have a well-fed appearance, have 'puppy fat' in fact, but not a distended or blown abdomen which denotes the presence of worms or wrong feeding, or even both. He should have a firm, solid feel to his little body. The skin of his abdomen should be pale pink and clean, without signs of scratching or any rash apart from the odd pimple caused by teething. Take a look at the hind legs to check if the hind dew-claws have been properly removed, assuming any were present at birth.

Quite a number of puppies do not have erect ears until they are five or six months old, some even later, but we like to see some movement forward and a sign of lifting when the puppy is on the alert. Beware of the very large ears that hang down like a pair of wet socks! If you decide on a puppy, ascertain when he was last dosed for round worms, and which product was used. Enquire about any inoculations he may already have been given, or which type the breeder recommends.

If you are choosing a companion puppy and are not greatly concerned with the finer points of a show specimen, do check for health in the same way. It is very distressing to take home a puppy, particularly as a family pet, and then to lose it through poor health or unsoundness soon afterwards. We feel that the greatest risk comes from cheap puppies advertised in local or evening papers. Some reputable breeders may advertise here, but most such puppies are offered by novice or pet owners, who may be kind enough towards their dogs, but simply do not have the knowledge necessary to rear a large and demanding family, and frequently lack the housing facilities, too. These pet puppies are often badly weaned and left on the dam too long without the supplementary feeding which is vital to a fast-developing breed such as the German Shepherd. This lack of proper diet can cause indigestion, rickets, poor bone and teeth and other handicaps to a growing puppy and bring costly veterinary bills to remedy them later on when the puppy has left for its new home.

If you are not in a position to attend dog shows or spend much time over inspecting litters, then your safest method to obtain a likely puppy is to ask the Kennel Club for a list of reputable breeders in your own area, or to buy the *Kennel Club Gazette* which publishes a list of breeders for each and every breed. In this way you may well find a nice one, and at least you have the guarantee of a recognized kennel and someone to come back to if you have any problems. (The address of the Kennel Club is to be found in the Appendix, page 172.)

We often tell buyers of our own puppies that we cannot, unfortunately, sell stock with a year's guarantee like a good watch, but we feel that recognized breeders will give the newcomer the best chance of a satisfactory transaction and be willing to give advice or answer questions concerning the puppy in its all-important early stages of development. For a German Shepherd Dog which is born weighing an average 16 oz and grows on to the adult weight of 65 – 70 lb (for bitches) and 70-80 lb (for dogs), it is evident that enormous quantities of food are necessary – something of which novice owners are not always aware. This is brought home to us when visitors exclaim at the large bowls of food served to our own dogs, and therefore we are reminded to press this point. It can thus be easily realized that a good start in life is of great importance, so be sure to ask your breeder for a complete diet sheet in advance of your actually taking the puppy away, if possible, so that you can have ready all the supplementary items. It makes the transition period easier for your puppy if he is not given unfamiliar foods which could upset his stomach and make it harder for him to settle in his new home.

If possible, obtain the registration certificate and pedigree when you collect the puppy. The Kennel Club is often somewhat in arrears with the issue of registrations, so they may not be available and through no fault of the breeder. You can, however, have the pedigree, with the details of the date of birth, etc. Some breeders offer a choice of names and many new owners are pleased to pick one from their list. You will require a transfer form to re-register the puppy under your ownership at the Kennel Club, and this must be signed by the breeder, too. Do try to complete all the formalities at the time of purchase. Dog breeders, even the best ones, are sometimes very unbusinesslike in their very full lives, and even move away so that you are in the difficult position of trying to trace them if you should require papers at a later date. So take your puppy and all the documents away together, or have the undertaking that they will follow as soon as they are issued by the Kennel Club.

6 About the First Year

With the purchase completed, you are all set to take your puppy home. We hope that you have given him an easy-to-call, simple name for everyday use – one or two syllables is ideal. Sometimes a name from one of his ancestors, taken from the pedigree, may strike your fancy. It is always fun naming any new baby, but in this case it should not be elaborate or difficult to pronounce, since you will use it often with a command, and it is best with a crisp sound. The registered name can be as imposing or striking as desired, of course. We always like to tell the story of a proud family who owned a dog whose registered name was the equivalent of Lord Princeling of the Upper Crust, but he answered to the name of Sausage! For the purposes of this book, shall we continue to call *your* puppy Bero?

Since small puppies are notoriously bad travellers, it is wise to make

Ten-month old bitch showing near adult development.

a few preparations for his first trip. A large cardboard box, obtained from the supermarket, with the bottom covered with a layer of torn-up newspapers and an old bath-towel over these, will furnish a temporary 'carry cot' with an absorbent layer. You can hold this on your lap if there is space enough, and it would ease the joltings of stopping and starting which tend to bring on vomiting. Have a box of tissues handy, as he may dribble and swallowing his saliva will only increase his discomfort. We shall be dealing in a later chapter with the whole question of travel sickness, here we are concerned solely with Bero's initiation into travelling at a moment when he is having to adapt suddenly to a whole set of new surroundings. We often find ourselves advising people taking their puppies away from our own kennels to drive as if they were conveying an elderly and wealthy but rather crotchety maiden aunt who was perfectly capable of 'leaving the lot' to the Cats' Home if she was upset! If a puppy is allowed to become miserable on his first trip in a car, you risk creating in him a phobia about car travel which may take a long time to eradicate.

Let the kennel know in advance the time you wish to call for the puppy, and arrive punctually having requested them not to feed him beforehand. A well-fed puppy will not take any harm from missing a meal if he is kept warm and out of draughts, and he will ride much more comfortably on an empty stomach. When the puppy is installed in your home, do keep visitors away from him for a day or two and restrain your own family – particularly young children who will be excited and want to make a fuss of the new pet. Just put yourself in Bero's place and imagine how confused and frightened he may feel at being the centre of attraction after the quiet routine life of the kennel. If he is overwhelmed by attention, however kindly, it may give him a complex of nervous reaction to humans for life. So take him quietly into your home, allow him to sniff around and talk to him quietly, giving him a drink of milk with warm water in which you have dissolved a teaspoonful of honey. Feed him his meat meal an hour later at least.

He will wander around, getting the answers to his questions from his own nose, and may well be anxious to attend to the wants of nature. So put some newspapers on the kitchen floor or outside in an enclosed yard, and leave him free to attend to his natural functions in seclusion. When Bero has had a meal and made himself comfortable he will feel sleepy, and his first requirement is a bed where he can rest undisturbed . . . remember that small puppies need a lot of sleep. It is a good idea to send a piece of blanket or a clean sack to the kennel, so that he sleeps on it for a night or two and it absorbs familiar odours which will help Bero to settle in his new surroundings. It is quite extraordinary how a youngster will turn to something which smells familiar, and relax quietly in acceptance of his new home.

For the bed itself, which needs to be large enough for him to stretch out on and is really more economical if it is bought of a size that will accommodate him when he is adult, we think that the commercial ones which are of canvas slung from a folding iron frame are perhaps the best for an indoor dog. These can be easily washed, and keep the puppy well out of the draughts along the floor. Those of our own dogs which sleep in kennels have wooden bench beds, on legs which raise them about 6 in. from the floor, with a good ledge along the front some six or eight inches high to hold back the wood-wool used for bedding. Blankets or sacks are equally suitable. This ledge is protected by a narrow strip of zinc sheeting formed over the top edge to prevent chewing; most puppies chew their beds, and while this annoys one terribly if a new bed is chewed and splintered by sharp young teeth, it is also worrying, since the puppy may have damaged his mouth or gums or swallowed a sharp splinter which could cause internal bleeding. If you prefer to wait for him to get over the teething and chewing stage before buying his permanent bed, you could bed him down very comfortably and cheaply in a large old tyre (the outer cover, that is) on a square of plywood and fill the centre with his bedding, not forgetting the comforting piece he brought from his puppy home. The tyre is proof against teeth, and effectively keeps out draughts as well.

When your puppy has been introduced to his new quarters and after his comfort and hunger have been attended to, leave him quietly with a large bone and some fresh water so that he can rest.

You will be wise to bring Bero home early in the day if possible, so that he has time to grow accustomed to his new surroundings and to yourself before nightfall. He will be lonely without his kennel companions and will miss the warm communal bed, and will probably make loud protests. You must be ready with firmness and patience. Put him back on his bed with his bone or some safe toy such as an old shoe or a thick rubber ring, and say encouragingly 'Good boy, Bero – Bed!', with emphasis on his name and the word 'bed'. Your tone of voice will help him to realize that bed is something pleasant, and that his toy is there and perhaps a small goody. In days to come you will only have to say 'Bed,' and he will understand that he has to go there at once, if you show patience to teach him this during his first few days in your care. Put some thick newspapers on the floor near his bed, as he is unlikely to go through the night without passing urine at this age. You may have to return to put him back to bed several times, but always do it quietly and firmly, praising him when he remains on his bed and making sure that he is not sleeping in a draught. Puppies always like to lie against a door, so if the weather is cold, put a mat or something thick and protective against any cold winds blowing under the door, on the other side so that he cannot drag it away and catch a chill.

You will have Bero's diet sheet and feeding times supplied by the seller, and you will have bought in the necessary items ready for his arrival. Do adhere to the kind of food and feeding times stated for at least a week, even if you disagree with them. It is unkind and foolish to take a puppy from his litter-mates and his early, familiar life and expect him to settle happily if his stomach is upset by strange food fed at different times. Be particularly careful with milk; if he has not hitherto been given cows' milk, give only small quantities until he is accustomed to it or he may have diarrhoea. Evaporated milk is usually accepted and digested well. Powdered milks are not high on our list, as they are prepared at such high temperatures that the virtues and values of the milk are largely destroyed. The addition of honey is always soothing and helpful to small stomachs.

Of course, as Bero grows he will not be so sensitive in his reactions to different foods, but during his teething periods he is quite likely to have digestive upsets. A teaspoonful of Milk of Magnesia twice each day, given before meals, will soothe his stomach ache. He will find unsuitable things such as coal, pieces of wood, stones and dirt to eat, and may chew up any articles he finds left around the house. New shoes and gloves are attractive and even your rugs – just the most valuable ones, of course! The best preventative for mischief of this kind is a good supply of toys of his own – a well-rinsed squeezy plastic bottle wrapped up in an old sock will amuse him endlessly as he 'undresses' his doll. Old shoes without laces or buckles, woollen socks and old gloves are all excellent. Never give *nylon* stockings for him to rip up; we nearly lost a puppy who swallowed a long piece of stocking and was very ill until it was removed by an oily enema and with much pain.

We have a great liking for health foods and much faith in them, both for ourselves and our dogs, and would like others to try the products that have earned our kennel a considerable reputation for health and stamina. Ours is such a natural breed, bred to live a healthy, active life out-of-doors where it thrives best. So let us feed our German Shepherds with as many of nature's best foods as can conveniently be found in present-day conditions of living. It will help them to live longer as healthy, happy companions, which is surely the goal we are aiming for, since their time here with us is always, alas!, too short.

We have mentioned several times that Bero is to be 'put' back on his bed or 'put' into the car, and this entails lifting him in your arms. As German Shepherds at this age weigh about 25 lb, it is just as well to learn how to lift him in such a way that his tender limbs and soft muscles are not damaged, nor he frightened by the pain that can be caused by inexperienced hands, however kind. Never allow anyone (nor do so yourself) to lift a heavy puppy by the scruff of the neck – this really

Correct way to hold a puppy.

hurts him, and he will feel that he is choking. Restrain him by grasping the loose skin round his neck, and meanwhile slip your other hand under his hind-quarters and grasp both his hocks, then lift him as he sits on your hand. In this way you will have control of Bero and he will be relaxed and comfortable. Moreover, with his weight thus properly distributed he is easier to carry about. We handle all our puppies this way and they enjoy being picked up and fussed, clamouring loudly for their turn when they are all together in the litter – time-wasting, perhaps, yet so worthwhile for their education, and for oneself, to have a few minutes fun in the long day of kennel chores.

House-training is your next problem. If you devote your time to this for the first week, you will be surprised how quickly Bero will learn to behave, but it does require watching and waiting on your part to anticipate his functions. Unless he can be whisked quickly outside at short notice, he must be trained to use a newspaper or a box of sand, or a 'cat litter'. Newspapers are highly recommended since they are easier for disposal. An average puppy in normal health has five or six bowel movements every twenty-four hours, most of which occur between 6 am and midnight; and he will urinate even more frequently. It is probably true to say that he will want to make a puddle immediately he wakes up from even a nap – the need to do so is the most likely cause of his awakening, in fact – and it is usual for a stool to be passed about ten minutes after feeding. So lift him outside and wait for him to perform, or put him on his newspaper and keep him there until it happens.

Sometimes it helps to leave a small bit of soiled paper from the previous time on top of the clean, as the odour will encourage and guide him as to where he should go. You will notice that Bero turns round several times before settling to do his duty. If he is not on his paper (assuming you have him indoors) put him there quickly, wait until he has finished and then praise him warmly. Don't praise him when he is in action, or he will amble towards you leaving a messy trail behind him. Both sexes squat to urinate at this age; males are about a year old before they start to lift a hind leg. Should he be caught *not* using his paper (or tray) indoors, show him the mess and scold him, but never rub his nose in it, as this only offends his dignity. Bero will soon learn from your voice: when he is in the right, then he is praised, and when he is in the wrong, then he is sternly reprimanded in a scolding tone.

We will repeat, one has to watch and wait. In any case, it is better to spend time and effort anticipating his functions than in the tedious cleaning-up afterwards. Should you discover one of his mistakes some time after it has happened it is useless to reprimand Bero as he will not have the slightest idea why you are angry. Anticipation, not correction, is really the keynote. Bero should be fairly closely confined until he can be trusted not to soil the floors. If you leave him the free run of the house, you will not be able to keep an eye on him, and he will be out of sight and out of range of his toilet facilities and may take advantage of it – something which can be quite difficult to break once the habit is formed. Ours is a very clean breed in its habits and prefers to use outdoor facilities. We are always hearing from pleasantly surprised owners, of puppies crying at the door to be let out, which proves how a little patience and time spent during the early days after his arrival will reward you greatly. Some trainers recommend that the puppy should sleep in an enclosed box, ventilated like a travelling-case, of course. This is done on the assumption that he will be unwilling, as most puppies are, to soil his bed. You will let him out straight on to his newspaper, or whisk him quickly into the garden, when he wakes up – or should I say, when you wake up!

If you can take Bero to your room for two or three nights, and are prepared to take him quickly and at once outside when you hear him stirring during the night, you will soon have him house-trained for all night. You may have to make three sorties the first night or two, and then twice will be enough, until he finally sleeps all night. This last formula depends a bit on the co-operation or tolerance of your human household concerning these nocturnal wanderings, although a week should be the fullest length of their duration. By then good habits should be established, and everyone can rest quietly all night. When your dog is fully matured and is fed one large meal daily, he will

Yearling bitch showing further development in backline and depth.

require a minimum of four exercising periods for health and comfort. The first early in the morning, the second about mid-day before his rest period (curiously, nearly all dogs sleep from 12 noon until 2 pm), again shortly after his feeding time and, of course, late at night before his bed time.

Dogs which are perfectly house-trained can sometimes misbehave to express resentment – at being left at home when they had hoped to accompany their owner, or when they have been disciplined, or to show jealousy. Our two stud dogs are excellent friends, but each morning they lift their legs against each other's kennels; and if one has a 'visitor' the other will sometimes break into the house and urinate against a door or table to show his jealousy. My beloved Chihuahua would climb upstairs on her tiny legs and drag down a heavy cover from my bed to make a puddle on, to show her fury at being left at home! One can only scold the offenders and try to keep them outside when there is any danger of misconduct, but when dogs who are house-trained urinate deliberately they do it for spite, and punishment cannot cure them – they will endure the scolding for the satisfaction of making the score even.

If your puppy has a mishap on carpeting, just mop up the surplus liquid quickly and then squirt a soda siphon on to the stain, drying afterwards with a clean towel. We have found this a good remedy for fresh stains, although it is no help at all with old-established ones. The worst outcome is the odour, which will attract Bero, or any visiting dog, back to the spot for misbehaviour. So take all care to banish any lingering smell. An air-freshening spray is useful, or a little ground coffee sprinkled on a hot shovel and wafted round the room. For very dirty messes, any of the various carpet shampoos will efface the traces in the majority of cases. In any event, clean up immediately you notice the trouble so that there is no danger of Bero being attracted by the smell for any future performances.

An unpleasant habit which shows up in puppyhood is that of devouring their own stools if these are not removed immediately. This is called Coprophagy, and it is never quite clear what causes it. Some breeders think it is brought on by some dietary deficiency, and it is true to say that when a vitamin supplement is given for a while the habit ceases, though it could be that it happens to coincide with the puppy growing out of this particular phase. Another, and perhaps more reasonable explanation, is that it is caused by indigestion (through teething or change of diet) so that the puppy passes undigested food which it is attracted to re-devour. The only sure remedy is to clean up quickly when Bero has 'spent his money'. As with all minor gastric disturbances, a small dose of Milk of Magnesia early each morning for two or three days will often end the trouble.

We mentioned that you should enquire from the breeder about worm dosing – when it was done and what product was used or recommended. Our own litters are first treated for round worms at 5-6 weeks and then again at three months. Two doses are given with a week's interval between them. The reason for this is that the round worm lays an egg which attaches itself to the intestine by a tiny hook, and is thus not expelled by the original dosing. These eggs will develop into worms during the next few days, but are not then old enough in themselves to lay eggs, so that the second dosing should make a clean sweep. If the puppy is given a dessertspoonful of liquid paraffin a couple of days after the second dose, it will avoid any chance of constipation or distress should the infestation have been severe. Quite often one sees a few worms, sometimes none at all. The modern remedies are usually based on piperazine or similar drugs, and are very efficient if given in sufficient quantities under veterinary instruction, but do not allow more than the week to elapse between the two doses. If you are in any doubt about your puppy suffering from round worms, you can ask your veterinary surgeon to test a stool. A very small quantity only is required, about as much as will go on a dessert spoon, and under microscopic examination the eggs are easily identified and diagnosis given. The specimen should be handed in to the surgery in a small glass jar, labelled with both your own name and the puppy's for easy identification.

The presence of worms can be suspected from any of the following symptoms: a swollen stomach after feeding particularly, when it can become distended out of all proportion to his body in severe cases; a slight cough, which is due to eggs in the aesophagus; watery eyes; and an erratic appetite. The chewing of stones and pieces of wood is sometimes suspected as a symptom, but is more likely to be the result of teething or indigestion. The next worm treatment is due at six months old. This is extremely important, with young bitches in particular, as expert veterinary opinion deems that if worms are thoroughly removed just before a young bitch first comes into season, she is less likely to infect her puppies later in life. The first period of heat can come at any time after six months, although more usually at eight months in our breed, so it is commonsense to give this matter your attention at the right moment.

We will return for a few lines to your puppy's inoculations. You will have asked the breeder if any have been given before taking Bero home. In some busy kennels a temporary immunisation is given at a very early age, and you should find out about this as it may affect the time suitable for his proper inoculations against Distemper, Hard Pad, Lepto-spirosis and Parvo-virus, these being the most dreaded and deadly of the diseases in dogs. Consult your own veterinary surgeon and obtain a certificate when the injections have been completed. This will probably be required if you have to put Bero in a boarding kennel at any time. On no account take your newly inoculated puppy to public places or amongst other dogs during the recommended period (usually ten days) of isolation. It is a wise precaution to take his temperature each day for three or four days afterwards in case of reaction or 'serum shock', although this is unusual in these days of highly perfected methods of inoculation.

The reader may feel that we have gone into the subject of Bero's early days in great detail, even that we have repeated ourselves at times. However, we make no excuse for the wealth of advice given as we feel sure that when the German Shepherd has crept into your heart as he has into our own, you, too, will feel that it is not too much, as everything one can do to help and protect this exceptional dog is a duty to everyone concerned in his welfare and his future. A healthy, well-adjusted animal will be your reward, and will be a source of pleasure and pride to you as his owner.

7   All About the Stud Dog

You may consider this only concerns the well-known breeder, but if Bero has a very good or interesting pedigree or if he has a few notable wins in the show ring, you may get enquiries – and feel encouraged to offer his services at stud. Unless you have already had some experience of this work it will be wise to witness some stud services, and if you are able to assist at the actual mating of two German Shepherds it will be very much to your advantage.

Ours being a slowly-maturing breed, it is normal for a dog to come to sexual interest later than several other breeds. We like to try a youngster when he is around fifteen months old to test his ability and his productive potential. However good he may prove to be, we do not like him to be in regular use until he is well over eighteen months. His eventual maturity and health may be affected by too great demands, and even the quality and size of his litters. If possible, find an older bitch with a reputation of being willing and easy to be served for his first attempt. The dog's whole stud career can be made or marred by his initiation, so it is well worth taking some trouble over the selection. Quite often no stud fee is paid or expected at a trial mating, although a puppy can be offered if there are good results.

Do not exercise Bero immediately before the mating; he really needs only a little very gentle trotting round some time before his visitor arrives, and, of course, he should not be fed a large meal either. If the visit has to be timed for the hour at which he is normally fed his main meal, give him an egg yolk beaten up with some glucose in half a pint of milk instead, so that he does not feel cheated of his meal. You can give him his meat when he has calmed down after the mating.

It is perhaps only right at this stage to mention that stud work is not nearly so rewarding financially as one could suppose. When a visit is booked to one of our dogs we make no other commitments for that day. The owner of the visitor usually arrives late or gets lost, has car trouble or similar hold-ups; and despite the instructions given, they frequently bring the bitch too early (see next chapter) or even too late! Do ask, when taking a telephone booking, that the owner exercises his bitch before reaching your house, so that she arrives empty and comfortable. This is a point which is often overlooked, and you will not want her to soil your own runs and excite all the dogs. If she seems thirsty or the weather is warm, do not give more than a large cupful of water.

Firm grasp of bitch at her mating.

Arrange for the mating pair to meet in a quiet and secluded place where they can get acquainted and do their courting, provided that the bitch is agreeable! Bero may become quite excited and nibble her ears and neck, play leapfrog and generally show off. A short exhibition is quite all right, but he must not tire himself too much. Take note of the way he goes about this overture and throughout the mating, as dogs seem to stick to a pattern for their stud work and a handler who knows and understands his dog is at an advantage. A wide strip of coconut or corded matting on the floor will prevent the dog's feet from slipping when he mounts and will make it easier to keep the bitch steady for him. Ask the person handling the bitch to grasp firmly at each side of her neck, standing face on to her, and to be ready to push her head between his knees to hold her steady so that she cannot bite or snap or throw herself down when the dog tries to penetrate her. You must remain at her side with an arm slipped underneath her loins, to prevent her from sinking down at her rear end at the important moment, which is an artful trick even maiden bitches practise.

Allow your dog several attempts to complete the act. Then, if he appears 'blown' or over-excited, put him on the leash and remove him outside or to his kennel for a few minutes, while the bitch calms down and everyone gets their breath back! If she is ill-tempered or very difficult, although quite ready for the dog in the strictly physical sense, she can be muzzled or restrained with a bandage over her jaws. Talk to the bitch soothingly and make sure that the owner does likewise. We have often found a bitch to be easier if held by a friendly handler, as the owner is apt to get over-anxious and upset, which is no help at all. If the visitor is a maiden, it is a good idea to smear round her genital parts, and just inside, with white vaseline on a sheathed finger, the handler holding her firmly meanwhile. Sometimes the dog will slip under or over the bitch and have a precipitate ejaculation. If this mishap occurs, let him stay mounted and continuing to make his mating movements, and it will not be long before he re-sheaths his penis. Taking him away will leave him extended for sometimes as long as ten minutes, in which case it is wiser, both for hygienic and safety reasons, to pass a piece of clean linen as a sling under his body to support him until he returns to normal. In this event, the dog should be rested for three or four hours before allowing him to make another attempt – in fact, the following day is better. Do not be alarmed by the discussion of the difficulties which may occur during a mating; most unions happen smoothly and comfortably for all concerned. However, it is only right that the owner of a stud dog should know what to do when things go wrong, also how to protect and assist the dog at his work.

Bandage firmly crossed under the chin and behind the ears to restrain the bitch at her mating – or any dog for veterinary attention.

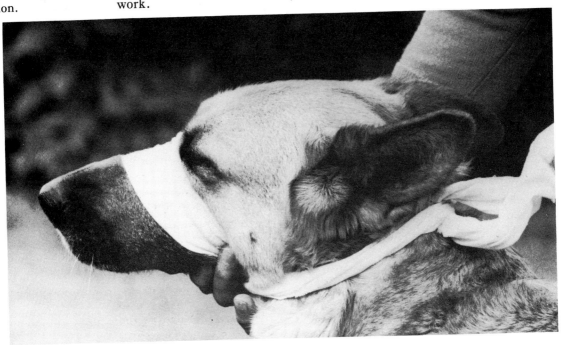

Having dealt with most of the likely problems, we can now continue with the normal procedure and assume that Bero has had a friendly exchange of sniffing and tail-wagging in courtship with his visitor. The handler is ready to hold her head steady, while you support her rear end, planting her hind legs well apart, and encourage the dog to mount. He will clasp his mate with his front legs bent round her waist and, so that you do not interfere with his hold, keep your supporting arm well back under her loins and see that her tail is kept over to one side.

When the dog has effected the union, he will move his hind legs in a stamping action, and you should support him on the bitch's back or alongside her for a minute or two before allowing him to turn round, as during this time he will swell inside her and arouse her muscular contractions to hold them both in what is termed the 'tie'. If he has difficulty in turning round, which is sometimes due to the bitch arching her back, you can gently guide his hind leg over her until he has turned completely. The two mates can then stand back to back in a natural position until the ejaculation of semen is completed, which can take from a few minutes to an hour, the normal period being about twenty-five minutes. The duration of the 'tie' has little to do with the size of the litter. We have had twelve puppies resulting from a brief encounter, and none at all from an hour-long one. Try not to interfere with the mated pair more than is necessary to steady them, but keep a sharp watch in case the bitch should try to roll over or lie down, when she could injure the dog. A stool or low seat for the person holding the bitch's head makes for comfort and ease of handling. When the dog withdraws, do not allow the bitch to run about or become excited, or to urinate, but take her quickly back to her kennel or the car to rest, and do not give her drinking water for half an hour.

The dog should also go to his own quarters to rest. If the service has been difficult or long drawn out give him a warm drink of milk and honey, or an egg yolk beaten up in warm milk, and leave him to recover before taking him for his daily exercise. Sometimes there is a request for a double service, perhaps because the bitch has been found to be difficult to get in whelp, or because she is growing old and a second service at a future heat would be unwise. If the dog is not heavily booked for services this could be allowed, but you must allow him several hours rest, as we mentioned earlier when contemplating a mis-happening.

The only worthwhile advertisement for a stud dog is the production of a good litter of sturdy puppies. So it behoves the owner to use patience and to give plenty of time to the visiting bitches in an endeavour to satisfy all parties concerned. However, no blame should be attached to a dog which has made strong efforts to mate a bitch without any success, there being any number of reasons for failure which have nothing to do with him. Perhaps the visit was made too soon or too late, or the bitch is a poor traveller and arrived in an upset condition. In spite of our advice, food *is* sometimes given and ample facilities for exercise are *not* given beforehand, so that there is physical discomfort. Another factor which governs the visitor's reactions more often than one would suppose is that she is so spoilt and indulged by her owner that she will not allow herself to be handled by anyone of the other sex – and sometimes not by anyone else at all!

To come to the business side of stud service. The stud fee or arrangement should be agreed *before* the service. Some owners will accept a puppy in lieu of a fee in money. If it is money, then it should be paid when the service has been effected and the dog's pedigree and registered number supplied. If a puppy is to be accepted, then the age when it is to be taken, whether it is to be first or second choice, whether dog or bitch, should be agreed between the parties, and a letter in confirmation written to keep matters in good order.

When you have a dog in regular use, it is convenient to have a small box at hand with the following items inside: a small tube or unbreakable jar of white vaseline; a thin, surgical-rubber finger sheath; a length of gauze bandage for muzzling, or a strong, comfortable muzzle which fastens securely; a large piece of clean linen in a plastic bag, in case a sling is required for the dog; paper towels or tissues; and a pair of thick, loose-fitting leather gloves, for handling sharp-tempered visitors. Other useful aids are a low seat or stool for easier handling during the 'tie' – and an abundance of patience and restraint.

We will finish this somewhat delicate chapter by saying that when patience, experience and good humour have failed to get the visiting female to co-operate and she persists in 'shrewish' behaviour, you can suggest that she be examined by the veterinary surgeon, who may find by exploration of the organs that there is some malformation or obstruction. If all is normal, a mild sedative is sometimes suggested. We feel that the dosage is best advised by the vet, as these products vary so much in strength and effect.

8 All About Breeding a Litter

This will be the longest chapter in the book, since it is the longest one in a breeder's life, and one which we feel is never completed. With thirty-six years' and approaching 200 litters' experience we are still learning and still thrilled with each expected litter. We dearly love our puppies and enjoy rearing them, making no other excuse for what could be considered as 'fuss' by some, but which we feel is essentially the right start in life for a dog as incomparable in beauty and intelligence as the German Shepherd.

Just as we advised when you were considering buying a German Shepherd puppy, we should like you again to stop and ask yourself a few questions before you embark on a venture which is as full of hazards as any which involves livestock, and, while it can be most rewarding, can be equally disappointing.

Breeding large dogs involves commensurate expense. The litters are usually large in numbers and need ample space, with ideally *two* kennels (one for day use and one for night use) so that the puppies have a dry, fresh house twice each day. Feeding is time-consuming as well as costly, and when the time comes to advertise your puppies for sale, this is also expensive. Then, if the litter is not all sold by ten to twelve weeks old you will have the expense and trouble of inoculations, and you will have to spend a lot of time training as the German Shepherd, with his highly developed outlook, cannot just be left in his kennel without lead training and some simple lessons for his future conduct. If he does not have some contact with the world about him, he will grow shy and withdrawn, and once this has happened it will be difficult, if not impossible, to rehabilitate him. So you must ask yourself if you are equipped to take on this considerable task and all that it involves. Then, if you are happy with the answers, we will go ahead.

We do not consider a bitch is ready to reproduce until her third heat, so that she will be round about two years old before her litter is born. Since our breed matures slowly, she will not have completed her growth and finish until this age, and will require her strength and substance for herself until she reaches the peak of her growth. In other words, she will have nothing to spare for a large litter of demanding babies, while the enormous strain of carrying a litter can affect an immature back and give it a 'dip' or make it soft and swaying for ever. A bitch must needs be in the pink of condition if she is to go through

The mature brood matron.

her ordeal, and then rear these large and greedy babies successfully. Our breed are notably good whelpers, with their roomy bodies and comparatively narrow heads. They also have an excellent reputation as mothers, and are careful and attentive with their families.

Your first step is the choice of a stud dog for her. If you are in touch with her breeders, you could ask what experiences they have had with her blood-lines and what dogs they consider suitable. You could also visit a few dog shows, and look for the type of dog you favour both in shape and character. Remember that type should match type, and take a few opinions before making your decision. Then try to work out the pedigrees, making a note of any dog that appears twice as this will mean that you are 'inbreeding' on this animal. This is not a fault in itself, indeed it is often a wise move, but it could prove disastrous if this particular animal carried an outstanding fault or major disqualification. All dogs have faults, but you have to bear in mind that you are looking for one to complement your bitch. Choose, for example, one which excels in hind-quarter angulation if your bitch fails here, or one that is noted for good shoulders and forechest, if this is her weakness. Above all, we beg of you not to even think of using even the most gorgeous dog if he has a faulty temperament or a nervous outlook. This would be sheer folly, even if your bitch has a perfect character.

The compensation of weakness with strength makes for successful breeding. However one *must* remember that in German Shepherd Dogs character ranks as high as conformation. From the sales point of view, too, this is important, as the pet buyer will fall flat for an engaging character lacking angulation, but will be disinterested in the trembling bundle of nerves which is teeming with show points.

When your choice has been fixed and you have asked if your bitch is acceptable, you must watch her carefully to see when she starts her heat and then notify the dog's owner at once, asking for a date twelve to fourteen days ahead to be reserved for you. Some other breeds mate earlier, but about fourteen days after the first show of colour is normal for ours, although bitches do vary quite a lot; we once owned one who never mated until the twenty-first day. However, once her date is reserved you can blot her vulva with a folded cleansing tissue or a piece of clean linen to note when the flow pales in colour and lessens in the volume discharged. Press your hand on top of her hind-quarters to test whether she will 'stand'. This is indicated by her planting her feet four-square and lifting her tail high or to one side. When you apply pressure to her hind-quarters she will brace herself and show pleasure if she is ready for the dog, often wagging her tail and whining with delight.

The period of acceptance of the dog is about thirty-six hours. Some bitches are 'ready' over a longer time, while others will last only a few hours. So you will see that it is only by trial and error that one learns which day to take her to the dog, but better too soon than too late, of course. If you do your part by checking her condition daily and informing the stud dog owner of her impending visit, you will find him co-operative, as all breeders are quite accustomed to this rather tiresome performance. If you have been giving chlorophyll deodorants and using an aerosol spray, you must discontinue both for a full forty-eight hours previous to the mating visit. Wash her 'pants and petticoats' with soapy water and dry thoroughly or the stud dog may be misled by the absence of the attractive sex odour and refuse to be interested in her.

Now, with the date settled, you will be off on your journey, arranging a morning visit if possible when the animals are fresh and their owners more relaxed, with time ahead for meals and the return journey. Do allow time for your bitch to be exercised and to perform all her normal functions before arriving at the kennels. If you can, let her urinate just before the end of the trip so that she is comfortable and less likely to fuss when the dog is with her. This is a really important point, but one that is sometimes overlooked by the uninformed or thoughtless owner.

We take a length (a yard is enough) of wide gauze bandage with us, in case the bitch is unwilling and tries to snap at her mate. The dog's owner will indicate how you can best hold her under control, but it is as well to muzzle her if there is any risk of her biting. Curiously enough, the sweetest natured bitches are sometimes positive shrews at these times, while a sharp one is charming and co-operative. As we have said, only experience will give the answers. Even so, it is to be noted that all bitches do not like all dogs, and yours may be happy enough with a different mate on a future occasion. We understand this behaviour, of course; what we find unacceptable is their strange passion for their brothers and fathers and other close and unsuitable partners, not to mention that 'wuffy' mongrel that comes along at these times!

When the mating has been effected, put her back in the car to rest and do not allow her to urinate for an hour, nor should you offer her drinking water unless the weather is very hot when you can just splash some in and around her mouth to refresh her. When you have paid the stud fee, obtain an agreement (usually written on the receipt) that you are entitled to a free second service if the bitch 'misses', which means that she has no puppies following this mating. Ask for a copy of the dog's blood-lines at the same time. Some well-known and much-used dogs boast a stud card, which is a printed and sometimes illustrated pedigree, which is very acceptable. However, in these days of extremely high printing costs, a breeder sometimes has to dispense with these niceties, which is a pity; but of course a luxurious stud card does not make a fine stud dog, so don't feel upset to receive a hand-written pedigree. With this step behind you, you can go forward to the stage of preparing your bitch 'to be a beautiful mother'.

Your bitch, whom we will call Anna for our mutual convenience, can follow her ordinary way of life for the next two or three weeks, as she is unlikely to show any signs of her condition yet. We are often asked at what age we start to condition our expectant mothers, the reply being 'as soon as they are born'! If Anna has been correctly reared and exercised all her life, she will not need any extra food or vitamins during her early pregnancy. Indeed, it is very unwise to overdo these things, which can make her overweight and also give her very big puppies, both of which can make for a difficult parturition.

Our breed, with their deep bodies, can hide their little secret for many weeks. However, her behaviour will let you know long before her contours change that she is expecting her family. Her increased interest in food, sudden drowsiness during the daytime, and a marked show of affection for her human family will be the earliest signs. Our own bitches become very close during their pregnancies, and it almost seems as if they cannot bear to have us out of their sight, which is as it should be as far as we are concerned. We feel sure that this trusting outlook has much to do with the perpetuation of good character and a friendly attitude towards the human race.

About the fourth week, Anna may become very hungry and will soon empty her dinner bowl. You can increase the meat ration by ½ lb now, but do not give any extra rusk or biscuits. Protein is her main requirement, and we do not want her to put on any soft fullness of condition, which is the result of increased starchy food. Give the extra meat in a small meal fed at mid-morning, and increase it by another ½ lb by the sixth week, so that Anna is getting 1 lb meat at 11 am and 1½ lb plus rusk, etc. at 4.30 – 5.00 pm. At six weeks, try her with a small early breakfast of one tablespoonful of semolina sprinkled into ½ pint of boiling water and cooked for 10 minutes. Cool this with either ½ pint of fresh milk or 4 tablespoons of evaporated milk, and add a large teaspoonful of honey. By the end of this week she will most likely take another semolina meal last thing at night. You will have to judge for yourself when to give this as the appetite can vary with the size of the expected litter, and while we are anxious not to overfeed her, she will suffer if she goes long periods without food. So four meals per diem is the rule from now on. She will be able to follow her normal pattern of life all through her pregnancy. Plenty of gentle exercise and fresh air are vital at this time, but no jumping or stunts of course.

Anna may start to beg for food now, which is part of the business of being in-whelp. You must resist her pleading as with four meals each day she is amply fed. A semi-sweet biscuit or a tiny square of plain cheese should be the limit of your indulgence if you feel compelled to yield, for she is not really hungry, just disturbed and uncomfortable in her digestion, which brings longings. Sometimes she may be comforted with plain or evaporated milk with water, with a little honey added, but never feed her baby foods or 'nightcap' milk foods, which are far too rich for canine use.

During the eighth week, you may find your lady-in-waiting starting to refuse her meals and to be very choice and fanciful about the food she wishes (or does not wish) to eat. At this stage you can pamper her and relax the rules slightly, without feeding really unsuitable tit-bits. You can cook some ox cheek or ox heart or a boned breast of lamb for a change of meat, or some carefully boned, cheap white fish mixed with raw egg after cooking is usually enjoyed, and a baked egg custard with honey or, instead, a few bits of boned chicken added. Do not allow her any bones from now onwards.

At this time the teats should have some treatment, to ease and facilitate the puppies' early feeding. Sponge her underneath with tepid water and some mild antiseptic soap, afterwards rinsing in clear water and drying her thoroughly. Now massage each mammary gently with a few drops of olive oil, to prevent soreness when the puppies start to suckle, and repeat this massage daily – no need to wash her again at present. About the 58th day a few drops of milk may appear, but you need not be concerned as it is quite normal and she is indicating that she is within two to three days of giving birth. About now we also like to trim her fur 'panties' around the vulva quite short, and also the underside of her tail to about half-way along. This makes for a cleaner, easier whelping, and one can better see if a puppy is lodged, too. Around twenty-four hours before her time she will suffer a sharp drop in temperature. If you have to give her fresh quarters for the event, Anna should start to sleep there some ten days before the great day. The whelping place should be high enough for an average person to stand up in, or you will find it difficult when feeding or cleaning out the premises. You can give her a meal in her new surroundings, and put a small seat in beside her so that you can stay awhile and read a book or talk to her, so that she is relaxed and familiar with her new home and accepts all happily. The most comfortable temperature for the whelping room is between 60 – 65°F. If it is too warm, Anna will be restless and may damage her puppies by moving around in her attempts to get comfortable, and if too cold the puppies will become chilled when she leaves them for exercise, or if one becomes separated during the night.

The method of heating depends entirely on where the whelping room is situated. Ideally, it is adjacent to the owner's house. Sometimes a conservatory or a verandah can be enclosed for the purpose, which enables frequent visits to be made and is convenient when the bitch starts to whelp in the middle of the night (and they usually do!). An infra-red lamp of the type used for poultry or pig breeding is excellent, and can be hung safely from the roof and over the nest so that the heat is evenly distributed and there is no danger of the restless, and sometimes distracted, little mother knocking it over. We cannot emphasize too much the terrible risk of any heating appliance on floor level or where the bitch could overturn it to cause a fire. When no heating is connected or when the weather is unusually cold, we heat clean bricks in the oven until they are very hot, wrap them in a thick newspaper, and put a couple in the whelping box with a piece of old blanket or a woollen garment over them. The puppies love this extra warmth, and will lie relaxed and contented beside the bricks, which gives the mother a chance to rest. Care must be taken that the babies cannot get behind the bricks so that they are unable to creep back to suck. These bricks are very little trouble, and if you have an Aga or similar stove you can keep a couple at the back of the oven always at the ready; they are safer than rubber hot-water bottles and retain the heat longer.

Some bitches urinate during the night at this stage, particularly if they are carrying a large litter, so it is wise to spread some newspaper down near her bed for possible use. You may have already had Anna examined by your veterinary surgeon during her period of gestation, so that he is advised of her date, but in any case it is as well to inform him and ask if he will be available at that time if required. These people take holidays or disappear on sailing or shooting adventures just when one needs them most, it seems. So make sure that someone is around who can help you. If it is someone that Anna already knows it will be all to the good, since she may not feel too well-disposed towards a total stranger when she is newly experiencing her maternal emotions.

The final item to prepare for Anna's happy event is the whelping box. As this may well be the key to her comfort and well-being, it is worthwhile taking some trouble over it, although actually it is a very simple affair which the average handyman can tackle. It should measure 4 ft or 4 ft 6 in. square (according to the size of her quarters) with back and sides about 7 – 8 in. high. It should have a removable front, of the same height overall, which slots in and is made in two pieces, so that when the babies are tiny only the lower half is left in position, while the upper half can be added to restrain them when they begin to roam at three weeks onwards. We fasten a metal band (tinned sheeting) around all exposed edges of the box, as bitches often chew anything handy if they are in pain or distress at the time of giving birth.

Inside the box, along the base of the walls, we screw three large metal cup hooks with rounded ends on each of the three fixed sides. These are not sharp, nor are they easily removed by the mother so they do not constitute a danger. Over these hooks we tightly stretch a clean, well-washed and rinsed sack which has been opened down one side so that it covers the entire surface. This makes a wonderful creeping aid for tiny feet to propel themselves back to the mother, and it is easily removed two or three times per day as necessary for the sake of hygiene. If the soiled ones are left to soak in a pail of detergent and water, then well rinsed, they soon dry for re-use. We emphasize rinsing well, as some animals have become extremely ill from licking in detergent-cleaned quarters – we even heard of a pony which died from this cause. Apparently there are ingredients in these products which are poisonous to animals, and as all animals clean their young with the tongue it is advisable to take special care in the maternity ward; carbolic soap is really the safest and best. During the time Anna is in labour and until the heavy discharge which follows the births subsides, keep thick newspapers under the sacking, which are easily slipped out and replaced as they become soiled. They give a little extra warmth underneath without any danger of a puppy becoming tangled up or lost in any loose bedding. One has to recognize that there is a lot of activity going on when the puppies are arriving, so that Anna needs ample room and an uncluttered box in which to manoeuvre herself and her puppies.

When the puppies are three weeks and older, Anna will leave them for longer periods as they grow more independent and begin to play amongst themselves, and it is now that they require cosier bedding, as they will often be sleeping alone and without the warmth of their mother's body.

We use a large piece of the artificial fur bedding (for example 'Vetbed' or similar type) to cover about one third of the box. We then put thick newspaper over the remainder of the box. Shredded newspaper can also be used as bedding; however it soon flattens down, and therefore it does not give the same comfort as the piece of 'fur' bedding.

It is important to provide the puppies with a warm and sheltered bed as they grow, so that the mother is able to rest contentedly away from them sometimes. Thus she is less likely to become bored with nursing and tending her litter. As well as the whelping box you will need a large, deep box or basket in which to put the babies while their quarters are being cleaned. Carry the box into the kitchen or a warm room where Anna can lie beside it. She will then soon accept the routine, and not try to return her babes to the whelping room by carrying them in her mouth, nor make a fuss and upset the puppies with her cries. If you put a warm brick in the box, prepared as suggested earlier in this chapter, the little things will soon be lulled off to sleep, while Anna has a peaceful nap to restore her. She will have half an eye open to watch her babies, nevertheless!

Now all is prepared for housing Anna and her family comfortably, we can revert to discussing her physical well-being and the actual birth of her puppies, always an exciting time in our own kennel and something we look forward to enormously. She should have her exercise for as long as she seems inclined to go out, but it is better to divide it into two spells now, so that she is not over-tired. Some bitches are eager to go out right to the last minute, and provided that they are accompanied by a capable and observant person there is no reason why they should not be allowed to have all the gentle walking they wish, as movement is good for them. With a strong, courageous breed such as ours, having a litter is something they take in their stride in most cases. Anna must not be left alone for long during the last week of her pregnancy in case she should be an early whelper, and also because some bitches become destructive at this stage and will tear up mats and cushions, if left indoors, in their anxiety to make a nest, or will dig huge holes in precious flower beds for the same reason.

For the actual birth day you will need a few useful items to hand in the whelping quarters. Place them on a shelf high above a dog's reach, but if this is not practical a flat basket suspended from the ceiling will serve your purpose. You will need (or may need) cotton wool, a pair of blunt curved scissors, a reel of white sewing silk, a small flask of brandy, a rectal thermometer, soft clean pieces of linen, two small Turkish towels, paper towels and a roll of sterile gauze. We take a small cardboard box (a shoe box is ideal) in with us when 'action stations' has been sounded, containing either a hot water bottle well wrapped in an old sweater, or a hot brick wrapped first in newspaper and then in a sweater. It is astonishing how a tiny puppy which appears to be lifeless can revive if it is placed in a warm basket at once. Don't forget a small notebook for yourself, in which you can jot down the arrival time and sex of each puppy and also its colour, making allowance for the fact that they are wet at this stage and may appear darker than they really are. Note any peculiarities such as one white foot or an especially large head and, of course, any abnormalities. These notes may be very useful for future reference.

Anna will probably alert you when her time arrives by an orgy of 'bedmaking' and fussing in her quarters, and will show a considerable swelling of the vulva and a discharge of mucus followed by muscular contractions of her whole body. The contractions begin as trembling spasms and increase in frequency and strength with obvious periods of sharp pain. Anna will pant rather alarmingly, and even cry or groan between these contractions. You must talk soothingly to her, and offer a small drink of milk, water and a teaspoonful of honey or glucose in case she feels the need for it.

The first puppy will be born within an hour of the contractions commencing, allowing for the variations in different bitches. The puppy comes into the world in a dark-coloured membranous bag, containing fluid. If the delivery has been reasonably quick and with no prolonged straining, leave the mother to attend to everything herself. Bitches are filled with instant wisdom and know-how at this moment, and one seldom has to worry over even the most flighty ones at this time. Indeed, we find that our gayest girls make the best brood bitches! If the puppy is not completely expelled and separated from the mother's body by the end of several contractions and some hard straining, take a firm but gentle hold of the bag in a small Turkish towel and carefully pull the puppy *downwards* and under the belly towards the front, making a gentle movement to coincide with the rhythm of her contractions. The normal presentation is head first, and in these cases all is usually straightforward for the bitch. Occasionally, a puppy comes out head last; this is known as a 'breach presentation' and the birth may well be difficult and prolonged. Here is where your assistance with the towel and gentle downward pulling will be of great help; but take great care never to jerk upwards, or you may cause a haemorrhage.

If the mother is tired after these difficulties, she may not immediately attend to the newly whelped puppy, so you must tear open the bag quickly with your finger and free the puppy's head, or it will suffocate. If the umbilical cord has been severed by the mother, you can rub the puppy fairly briskly with the towel to make it cry. However, if Anna is still too exhausted persuade her to lie quietly for a few minutes rest, and when she has recovered she will most probably lick the puppy vigorously to get the circulation going, then bite through the cord and devour the afterbirth (or placenta, as it is sometimes known). The short quiet period is also useful in the case where you have to sever the cord yourself, for as soon as the puppy is born the flow of blood through it to the placenta diminishes rapidly so there is less risk of any severe bleeding. Snip the cord with your blunt curved scissors (which have previously been wiped with weak Dettol), holding them on one side so that they crush the cord with their bluntness, and this will stop the bleeding. Make the cut about 1½ in. from the puppy's belly. If by some mischance the cord should bleed profusely, you must tie it with a double piece of the sewing silk from your first-aid kit and put one tiny drop of disinfectant on it.

There are two schools of thought about the disposal of the afterbirth. One holds that it is normal and natural for bitches to devour them all, while the second holds that this is quite wrong and encourages cannibalism. The first theory is founded on the belief that the afterbirth helps to cleanse the mother and bring the milk. The second is dead against the bitch being allowed to clean up after the birth both on hygienic grounds and because of the possibility just mentioned of her devouring the puppy too. We rather tend to take the middle course and allow her to attend to some, while we remove the others swiftly with a newspaper, when they must be burnt immediately. We have noticed that if all are left with her it can bring on violent diarrhoea, evil-smelling and unpleasant in the kennel, even if not in itself harmful as it soon clears up.

Should a puppy appear lifeless, do not immediately give up hope. After a brisk rub with the towel, wipe the mucous out of its mouth with a small piece of the sterlized gauze, grasp it in the towel and swing it gently head downwards a couple of times when it may decide to cry and breathe. If this fails, cover its mouth with your own and breathe in and out rhythmically in the 'kiss of life', then wrap it warmly in something woolly (old sweater sleeves are fine) and put it on top of the hot water bottle; warmth works wonders with puppies.

The puppies may continue to arrive at intervals of anything between a few minutes and an hour, and may be as many as twelve or as few as two or three. We have experienced the disappointment of a solitary baby from a mother who was large and promising, and the shock of seventeen from a mother who did not appear any larger! Should there be longer than two and a half to three hours much hard straining after the latest birth, it is time to get your veterinary surgeon to help. You may find your little notebook useful here to supply the answers to any of his questions about times of first delivery, intervals between puppies and so on.

Meanwhile, you will have been offering small drinks of milk and warm water, with either honey or glucose added, between each birth. Also, if you keep a box of semi-sweet biscuits handy (such as petit beurre or digestive sweet meal) she will probably accept a few after the arrival of two or three puppies and when there is a lull in the activity. The majority of bitches welcome the quiet presence, and the praise and endearments, of their owner or a well-liked attendant during their ordeal, and, of course, one feels easier in one's mind if allowed to be in beside the mother, keeping a vigilant eye on everything. However, we are bound to say that there are some brood bitches who are affectionate enough in everyday life, but when they are giving birth they prefer to be left alone and may even say so quite plainly and chase you out! In this case, put down plenty of thick newspaper on the floor, and a large shallow dish of the milk and honey mixture, see that she is warm enough, and then leave her to her own devices. Somehow an independent or even somewhat aggressive bitch never seems to need any help with her litter's arrival, and in the event of something going wrong she is usually intelligent and wise enough to permit a helper to enter the kennel.

The birth period may extend over twelve to eighteen hours if the litter is large. So during this time slip a lead over Anna's head and coax her to go outside and relieve herself a couple of times, and again when all is over. She will be more comfortable if the bladder is kept empty, and it is good for her to make some movement, too, even if she walks only a dozen yards. During the birth, there may be intervals of an hour or so when Anna will take a nap and rest from her constant licking and investigating of her babies, and you can safely leave her alone. The vigorous licking is done to keep the circulation going and to encourage the babies to urinate.

When Anna has finished whelping, you may notice that she is sleepy and relaxed and inclined to stay close to her puppies. If you have any doubts that there may be another puppy still to come away, then ask your veterinary surgeon to call and check up thoroughly. You may have to slip a gauze bandage over her muzzle during the examination, as she will be tender and may not welcome a stranger handling her. You can now wash her 'pants and petticoats' with warm water and some pleasant germicidal soap, drying her thoroughly with a warm towel before putting her back again. Remove all papers from her quarters, keeping the puppies in their warm box meanwhile, and wipe over the whelping box with a cloth sprinkled with Dettol or a similar product, putting down thick, clean paper when it has been wiped dry. A final warm drink for the tired mother (perhaps one for you!) and she can be left to rest blissfully and proudly tend her babies. You will not, of course, allow her to be visited or peered at by other members of the family for two or three days, or she may be alarmed and devour her young in her distress.

Keep Anna on a light diet for the first twelve hours. A couple of fresh egg yolks, beaten in a cupful of boiling water with a cupful of fresh milk plus two tablespoonsful of evaporated milk, and with two crushed calcium tablets added, may be given. Or soaked barley kernels and a little clear chicken broth (jellied) is tasty. The calcium is essential at this phase, eight tablets per day for the first week and afterwards six – that is three each in breakfast and supper. This is most beneficial in replacing her own lost calcium and in steadying the flow of discharge from the uterus, and also as a general boost for the condition of both mother and babies.

The following day, put her back on her semolina breakfast and supper, adding the crushed calcium and fresh or evaporated milk. For lunch give her 1½ lb freshly cooked white fish with a couple of large spoonfuls of evaporated milk and two crushed calcium tablets added. Feed her a small amount of fresh meat, say 1 lb, in the early evening of this first day, but do not feel alarmed if she refuses it and prefers the fish again; some bitches do not relish meat for two or three days after whelping. You can give her small drinks of milk and water between meals for the first eight or ten days, when the puppies are totally dependent on her and with their rapid growth are making heavy demands. We make one visit during the night for the first few days or until the mother is really settled to her routine, and we leave a shallow dish of milk, honey and water beside her box for the night. All this sounds like a lot of work – and indeed it is. However, it was your idea that Anna should have a family, and now you must share the responsibility of caring for it! Some may think we sound fussy, too, to which our reply must be that they do not know how fascinating our pretty puppies are in the nest, nor how much enjoyment is experienced in rearing a litter. One feels compelled to give them full attention and care in return for the fun.

Anna's programme during the nursing period will be as follows, although quantities are approximate, since more food may be required if she has, say, eight puppies and less if the litter is small. Her appetite will also guide you, as this is a time when she may have her fill of good food. The puppies will benefit from her ample meals and she will not be so hungry when the weaning commences, so you can restrict her

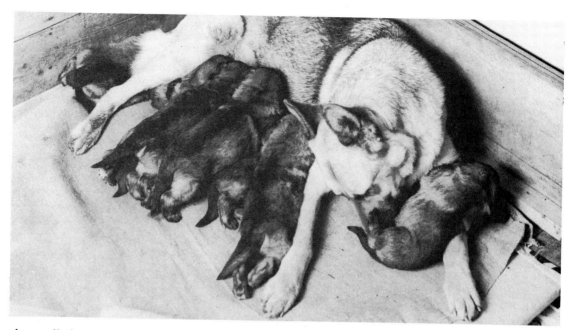

then a little for her figure's sake. Anna should be fed six times per day for the first month, after which time she will be nursing her litter for short periods only and at night. Consequently her diet should contain less milk, as she is actually starting the weaning period.

Mother's devoted attention while hefty four weeks old puppies enjoy their breakfast.

Our own system is to give warm milk and water early, when she is let out to exercise. Meanwhile her quarters are tidied up and soiled papers removed, the puppies are inspected, the heating checked etc. When the bitch is back and comfortable with her babies, we give the semolina breakfast. At 11 am she has a meal of 2 lb fresh meat with a teaspoonful of olive oil and a tablespoonful of grated carrot. At 2 pm ½ pint of fresh milk or four tablespoonsful of evaporated milk with warm water and a teaspoonful of glucose or honey, plus two or three semi-sweet biscuits if she seems hungry. At 5 pm we give 1½ lb fresh meat, a small handful of rusk or meal and seaweed powder, or whatever additive she normally has on her food. At 7 pm she has a milk meal as at 2 pm, and last thing at night, a semolina drink as at 7 am. You can vary Anna's times to suit your own way of living, but try to keep the same regular intervals between meals, and let her come out for exercise and a rest from nursing whenever she is inclined and you can spare the time. The idea of these frequent sorties is to avoid boredom for the bitch. For if she has been accustomed to go about with you or to lie about the house she will be feeling lonely now you go out without her.

When her litter is four weeks old, stop the 2 pm and 7 pm milk feeds, taking two or three days to reduce them until you cut them out altogether. Reduce the 11 am meat to 1½ lb during the fifth to sixth week, and during the sixth to seventh week give smaller quantities of semolina and milk until she is only having a saucerful night and morning, as the puppies will be weaned by now. Give the two meals 1½ lb of meat each time, without any rusk or meal until the milk dries up. If you spread the reductions over two or three days, Anna will not feel deprived or hungry, since the puppies' demands are also less as the days pass. Start her daily walks at six weeks, and by the time the puppies are eight weeks old she will be more or less back on her normal diet, although we allow a few extras to aid the recovery from the strain of nursing. Some bitches give everything to their puppies, and come out of the nursing period like skeletons, while others are less yielding to their babies, and look quite normal in coat and condition afterwards.

If the milk still persists, you can give a *small* teaspoonful of ordinary Epsom Salts first thing in the morning for a couple of days, which helps to dry it up. Anna may like to visit her babies once or twice each day after they are weaned, and this should be allowed, but keep the visits brief, as the babies will suck and stimulate the milk flow. However, as most bitches enjoy their maternity it will keep Anna happy if she can make an occasional inspection, and it also comforts the puppies whose character usually reflects the mother's disposition. Therefore, one happy mother = happy babies plus some amusement for ourselves, as we enjoy seeing them play together.

When Anna is completely separated from her family, you will want her underline to firm up again, especially if she has a show career to

Drying off the milk after weaning with a saucerful of methylated spirits (or surgical spirit) and olive oil.

resume. We use a large saucer filled with a 50-50 mixture of olive oil mixed with methylated spirit or surgical spirit, which we hold underneath her and gently dab on her mammary glands, repeating daily for two or three days. The spirit dries up the milk and shrinks the teats, which are kept soft by the oil to prevent painful cracking. If there are any scratches or tears from the puppies' claws, cover these first with a little white vaseline. If conditions are suitable, a good bath as soon as convenient after the separation is very necessary. Dry her well and keep her very warm.

9   All About Puppies from Birth to Weaning

We have seen our brood bitch through her ordeal until weaning time, and now we return to the whelping day to start rearing our puppies. During the first few days Anna will be very possessive, and if you have to attend to a puppy or remove a dead one, just drop a towel over it, when it can be lifted out under cover so that the mother is not distressed. Should any puppy seem not to prosper at once, it can often be revived by removing it to a warm place. We have even put puppies for a few minutes in the warming oven of the Aga, keeping the door ajar, and feeding it gently with a little warm boiled water and glucose in the proportion of one teaspoonful of glucose to ¼ pint of water, using an eye-dropper. It can be returned to the nest when restored.

Now is the time to weigh your litter and to make a chart to record their weights for the first three weeks, so that you can easily check on progress. If you note markings or anything else significant about each puppy, you will soon learn to identify them from the constant handling and watching over them, even if at birth they are as alike as the ten little nigger boys.

Concerning the size of the litter, this is governed by several factors. Ideally, six puppies on a maiden bitch and eight on a mature matron is the best number. Most bitches have eight teats which function. The hind ones are the largest and have the most plentiful supply of milk, and you may notice that the earliest arrivals in the litter go straight to these and stake their claim by holding on against the pushing tactics of newcomers. This is the reason why six puppies are considered sufficient, as the first teats near the front are small and less well supplied, and unless you are prepared to be in the whelping place frequently to change the positions of the sucking puppies, someone is going to be hungry and will grow weak and not be able to fight for the generous end of the 'bar'. We make a point of changing over the puppies from one end of the row of teats to the other whenever we see a greedy one forging ahead at the expense of a smaller brother or sister, for these early days are vitally important, although a small but strong puppy will usually catch up in growth when the weaning begins in earnest.

We have to make allowances for nature who can step in (and usually does!) to alter our own plans. You may have the problem of twelve puppies on hand on day one; it will do no harm to mother or babies, provided that the births have been normal, if you allow thirty-six hours to pass before making any decision about the surplus babies. One or two weakly ones may fade or show some small abnormality which makes the decision about their disposal easier; white ones should be destroyed in any case. If you have any puppy sales already arranged, you will have to consider sex in that context when weeding them out. A balance is best as a rule – an equal number of lady babies and laddie babies!

The time when your veterinary surgeon calls to remove the dew-claws (if any) is the appropriate moment to go through the litter and decide how many you are keeping. The dew-claws are the large ones on the inside of the hind legs which stick out like the thumb on a human hand. They must be removed carefully and thoroughly or they can give a clumsy appearance and even impede a dog's hind action by catching on things. Your veterinary surgeon will remove them swiftly and with little pain at four days old, and the mother will lick them to hasten the healing of the little wounds. She must be kept well out of hearing during the operation, and it is well to keep an eye on her for a short while after they have been returned to her, in case the smell of their blood excites her. Do not forget to remind the vet that only the *hind* dew-claws are removed on our breed – the front legs are not touched. Quite often, as a result of the evolution of the dog, hind dew-claws are not present which saves a lot of trouble. Their presence, however, is not a fault, the dew-claws being originally intended for fastening onto their prey when caught after the hunt, and now being more or less redundant.

The first two weeks of your puppies' lives are the easiest for all concerned. The mother will be recovering from whelping and proudly tending her family, which apart from the constant cleaning of their quarters and the feeding and exercising of their mother will not trouble you with extra work. But once their eyes are open (at between twelve and fourteen days) your many duties will begin. If the eyes are not effectively cleansed by the mother, you can bathe them with cool boiled water and a bit of cotton wool. This is the time to start the puppies on raw meat, which is their natural food. It should be lean fresh beef, shin or chuck steak being the best. Perhaps this may seem extravagant, but it is only for the first week or so – afterwards, horsemeat may be given. Scrape the beef with a sharp, heavy-bladed knife onto a board, carefully removing the sinews and bits of skin and gristle. Put about a ¼ teaspoonful on the tip of the finger, and gently work it into the puppy's mouth. Many puppies will take it greedily at once and pull on your finger, asking for more. Others can be very slow, and will 'mouth' this new flavour and texture, and you may have to persevere for two or three feeds before they accept it, but with patience you will soon have

Left: 'Please be kind!' The irresistible look of a three weeks old puppy.

Below: 'What's this stuff?' Three weeks old puppies investigating their porridge.

them all eating eagerly. Put them back onto their dam afterwards to suckle, as this helps their digestion. Feed the meat to the little ones once on the initial day and twice on the six days following; mid-morning and mid-evening are the times they will best accept the meat. You should progressively increase the quantity until they are taking a tablespoonful at each feed at the end of the week.

At three weeks you can teach them to lap. This is another exercise in patience and perseverance for you, and a time-consuming one, too. You will, in fact, have to be ready to give lots of time to the litter for the next few weeks, which are very important to them, as you will see from the recommendations which follow. We usually spread a clean newspaper or a plastic sheet down on the kennel floor, so that sawdust (if used) or bedding do not get mixed in the food to cause indigestion. Have ready in a jug a mixture of half milk and half water, or two tablespoonsful of evaporated milk to a ½ pint of water, with a small teaspoonful of honey, plus – for each puppy – half a tablet of calcium or bonemeal crushed up. With this jug and a large and shallow dish you can now go into action. Group the puppies around the dish, and gradually pour in a little liquid, putting your fingers in and encouraging the babes to suck and lick their new food. Here again, you may find that some puppies lap easily while others seem displeased at their change of diet! Be very careful that the liquid is not more than blood heat (about 101°F) or the greedy may lap it quickly and burn their tender mouths, which will set them back in their weaning. Give this milk mixture (about a pint in all, plus the honey and calcium at the rate of half a tablet, crushed, per puppy, should satisfy the average litter) early in the morning and last thing at night, which helps Anna with her nursing programme as this is, by now, diminishing.

Alert and watchful already at four weeks old.

With your litter now four weeks old, you must be prepared to take over from Anna, who will stay with them at night and be on guard and interested in her babies but yet, as nature has decreed, will be withdrawing her attentions and preparing them to face the world on their own. The puppies' claws will have grown quite long white tips which are extremely sharp and will need cutting if they are not to cause pain and distress to Anna. Use sharp scissors with rounded ends and clip the tiny tips quickly, and if you have the misfortune to cut a small toe, dab it at once with iodine. This nail trimming must be repeated about every ten days until the weaning is completed, so that the puppies do not tear their mother when nursing, particularly in this 'standing' position when she is most vulnerable.

During the puppies' fifth week, you must introduce them to their cereal foods. Make semolina porridge, as you have been doing for Anna, and dilute it well with fresh or evaporated milk, adding the essential honey and calcium in the rate of a whole tablet each time for each puppy. They are now teething and growing fast, which requires every assistance one can give to make them sturdy, 'chunky' young-sters. They can have some bread or rusk mixed in with their meat now. We use wholemeal bread crumbs, or wholemeal bread finely crushed after it has been dried in the oven to a crisp, biscuity rusk – *not* toasted,

Suckling four weeks old puppies in the 'standing' position.

which makes a soggy texture when soaked in broth. You can also start to mince their meat with the fine cutter, carefully taking out any gristle and pulping it with the heavy knife to make sure it is not stringy, which could cause choking. Their menu at five to six weeks should be as follows (all quantities are for one puppy):

7 am: ¼ pint semolina porridge, with four tablespoonsful of milk or 2 tablespoonsful of evaporated (thinned with an equal quantity of water), one small teaspoonful of honey, one calcium (with Vitamin D) or bonemeal tablet crushed up.

10.30 am: 2 oz pulped raw meat, one tablespoonful of oven-dried crumbs soaked in broth, ¼ teaspoonful of olive oil, ¼ teaspoonful of very finely grated raw carrot.

4.30 pm: as at 10.30 am.

10.30 pm: as at 7 am.

The increases must be made very gradually until the puppies are taking the full amount. If any food is left over, throw it away, as it will quickly turn sour and upset the puppies' sensitive digestions. Keep Anna away from her litter for at least an hour before each of their meat feeds, so that they are hungry and eager to eat. Also, take care that she does not rejoin them to help eat their rations; bitches are very 'bound up' with their young and it is something of a task to keep them apart when weaning time comes, although there is always the exception who 'could not care less' and may cause you even more anxiety by rejecting her babies quite early. However, once they are one month old you can always feed them adequately if need be, and successfully rear a sturdy gang. In these cases, a raw egg yolk (one between two puppies) can be beaten into the milk feeds for extra nourishment.

The puppies are now six weeks old, and due for the very important dosing for round worms. These are present in a varying degree in all puppies; they are not the result of any negligence on the part of the breeder, so do not feel upset, even if the babies are heavily infested. The real anxiety is to purge them away quickly and completely, as no puppy can thrive if these parasites absorb the nourishment so vital to rapid growth. Hence, the greatest care must be given to the necessary medication. Weigh two or three puppies, and ask your veterinary surgeon for doses for the *average* weight. Should there be a very small puppy, treat him individually, of course.

Give the worm dose early in the morning and follow it with the warm porridge. We prefer to dose each puppy individually, by putting the pills down his throat, as if the dose is crushed and added to the food the puppy which eats least will get the smallest dose, and vice versa. The dose should be repeated six days later – we have dealt with the reasons and given a full description in the chapter on the First Year. If the puppies are distressed or constipated one or two days after the dosing, give a small teaspoonful of liquid paraffin to ease and soothe the intestine, which can be disturbed by the departure of the parasites. With modern medications, one can see the round worms in the stools up to forty-eight hours after dosing, so do not be alarmed if these should appear when you think that all is over. At the second dosing, you may not see any signs at all, but the larvae will have been destroyed, which is the object of this repeat dose.

By this time, Anna will be providing very little, if any, of their nourishment, but you will find it comforts the babies if she will go into bed with them even for a few minutes last thing at night. You can also allow her an early morning visit, once she has decided to sleep away from them, or even a couple of times during the day, as bitches generally like to play with their babies at this stage. Indeed, their antics are very amusing, and we regard the fun they give us as a small reward for the long weeks of care and attention. When the weaning is nearly completed the puppies will be thirsty, since they have not yet learned to drink enough water for their needs. We give a large bowlful of warm milk and water — half and half — with a little glucose added at 2.0 pm and 7.0 pm, between their main meals, until their little stomachs are capable of taking on larger meals and they learn to drink water — usually about the tenth week.

We now give some points for your guidance, since the litter is entirely under your care from this time onwards. To save time, you can make one single large brew of porridge at night, and either put the morning rations in a Thermos jar, so that you only have to pour it out and cool it for their breakfast, or leave the breakfast portion in the saucepan and warm it by adding hot milk in the morning. The honey and calcium are best added at the time of feeding, in either case. You can also prepare a whole day's meat supply in the morning, and leave the second portion in a cool place until feeding time comes round again. Do not refrigerate, as very cold meat can cause colic or diarrhoea. Avoid a high percentage of fat in their meat, and always feed their meals at blood heat. Remove all left-over food from their kennel or pen if it is not eaten up within an hour, and reduce the quantities for future meals until all is cleared-up at once. Puppies are no different to ourselves and do not always feel like a hearty meal, particularly when they are teething or when changing routine upsets them. However, if poor appetites persist, and also if other symptoms are noted such as listlessness or diarrhoea, call in your veterinary surgeon at once.

Give only very large marrow bones or 'H' bones, so that there can be no splinters to cause damage to tender mouths — or even worse damage if they should be swallowed. These bones should always be either well-boiled or baked in the oven, as raw ones soon become maggotty and will upset their stomachs. Bones are very good as teething aids and help to form strong jaws; if given after meals they encourage the gastric juices and make for a good digestion, and, of course, they are most useful to keep a lonely puppy quiet if he has to be left, and also to settle one at night.

Beware of excess dosing of vitamins and additives in an effort to force the puppies' growth and condition. This is really dangerous and causes an imbalance of food intake, and if calcium is given in over-large doses this can cause calcium abscesses. Feed at regular times, and keep all feeding utensils scrupulously clean.

If the puppies have to be mainly in their kennel owing to weather conditions, you will need a thick sprinkling of sawdust on the floor to absorb the messes, as Anna will no longer (and indeed should not) clean up after them. You will need to change this up to half a dozen times a day, depending on how often and for how long they can go outside. Their furry bedding will also have to be changed morning and evening while they are so young. When they start to go outside, at about one month old, give them a large box in a sheltered spot, or put it on its side, so that the puppies are cosy and can get out of the wind and sun. German Shepherds usually dislike the hot sun, so protect your puppies with a shady spot for their rest bed. They must never be allowed to lie about on cold stones or concrete or the damp

Hear no evil, see no evil, speak no evil. The wisdom of 100 years as a dog in service to mankind shows already in the eyes of these four weeks old puppies.

earth, or they will soon have chills and rheumatism.

If you have to spray the puppies for fleas, cover the nose and eyes with an old handkerchief or a piece of gauze meanwhile, as these organs are extremely susceptible to pesticides.

Finally, beware of visitors! Make it a rule that no young children, and as few adults as possible, are allowed to pick up the puppies. A small limb can easily be dislocated, and a heavy puppy dropped by unskilled handlers with the result that its back or head can be permanently damaged. It can be made hand-shy, or wary of children, all its life, if it is frightened or hurt at this stage. Even puppies with the best of temperaments are very sensitive when small, and can suffer a severe set-back, at the very least, from being wrongly handled. It is not fair to others who come to buy a puppy, if earlier visitors come inside and pull it about, however well-meaning they may be, and this is a point you can put to callers who are full of good intentions but are hard to convince. In other words, it is the slogan of the fruiterer who labels his soft fruits 'Don't Squeeze Me Until I'm Yours'!

10 All About Weight and Dieting (Puppies and Adults)

We print overleaf a table of weights, taken daily, from birth to the end of the third week, of a litter of eight normal puppies, born naturally from a champion sire and a prize-winning bitch, and thus with the perfect background for an average litter in size, conformation and type. You will notice from it how level the progress has been, even with the small ones; they gain weight in step with the biggest, and the table shows an average increase of 1 lb per week. The increase is even greater when they are weaned, and at eight to nine weeks you can expect your dog puppies to weigh between 12 lb and 14 lb and the bitches around 2 lb less. Much of this weight is bone, as ours is a heavy breed. You will have been feeding calcium and other foods which produce good bone, an essential in an active dog. Curiously, some fat, soft-fleshed puppies, fed on starchy and fatty foods, are not so heavy as the big-boned, sturdy, 'dry-fleshed' ones.

This four weeks old puppy seems surprised at her rapid increase in weight.

DAY-BY-DAY SPECIMEN TABLE OF WEIGHTS
(In pounds and ounces)
FOR THE FIRST THREE WEEKS

BITCH 1
No dew-claws
No white on chest
Slight white toes on
  back feet
Birth weight 1.4

WEEK 1	1. 9	WEEK 2	2. 8½	WEEK 3	3.10½
1. 4½	1.11	2. 3½	2.11½	3. 1	4. 0
1. 6	1.12	2. 5½	2.14½	3. 4	4. 3
1. 7	1.14½	2. 9½	3. 0½	3. 6½	4. 7½

BITCH 2
Dew-claws
White chest
Slight white toes on
  back feet
Birth weight 1.2

WEEK 1	1. 8	WEEK 2	2. 9½	WEEK 3	3.13
1. 3½	1.11	2. 4½	2.12	3. 3	4. 2
1. 5½	1.13	2. 7½	3. 0	3. 6½	4. 5
1. 5½	2. 1	2. 8½	3. 0½	3.11	4. 8

BITCH 3
Black face
No dew-claws
White toes on left
  back foot
Birth weight 1.1

WEEK 1	1. 7	WEEK 2	2. 9	WEEK 3	3. 8
1. 2½	1.10	2. 1½	2.11½	3. 1½	3.10
1. 4	1.11	2. 3	2.13½	3. 2	3.12
1. 5½	1.13	2. 7	3. 0½	3.5	4. 0

DOG 1
Dew-claws (1 double)
No white on chest
White toes on left
  back foot
Birth weight 1.2

WEEK 1	1. 9½	WEEK 2	2. 9	WEEK 3	3.11
1. 3½	1.12	2. 2½	2.13	3. 3	3.14
1. 5	1.14	2. 5	2.12½	3. 4½	4. 1
1. 6	2. 1	2. 8	3. 0	3. 8½	4. 3

DOG 2
Dew-claws
Slight white chest
Slight white toes on
  all feet
Birth weight 1.4

WEEK 1	1.12	WEEK 2	2.10½	WEEK 3	3.13½
1. 6½	1.13½	2. 5	2.14	3. 4	4. 2
1. 8	2. 0	2. 6½	2.15	3. 7	4. 4½
1. 9½	2. 2½	2. 7½	3. 0	3.11½	4. 9

DOG 3
Double dew-claws
White chest
White toes on back feet
  and front right foot
Birth weight 1.3

WEEK 1	1. 9½	WEEK 2	2. 8½	WEEK 3	3. 9
1. 3½	1.11	2. 3	2.11½	3. 2½	3.14
1. 5½	1.14½	2. 4½	2.13	3. 4½	4. 2
1. 6½	2. 0	2. 5½	3. 0	3. 7	4. 7

DOG 4
Dew-claws
Black face
White chest
White toes on back feet
Birth weight 1.0

WEEK 1	1. 7	WEEK 2	2. 7½	WEEK 3	3. 6
1. 1½	1. 9	1.15½	2.10	3. 0½	3. 9
1. 3½	1.12	2. 4	2.12½	3. 3	3.13½
1. 4	1.14	2. 4½	2.14½	3. 4½	4. 0

DOG 5
No dew-claws
Slight white chest
Black face
No white toes
Birth weight 1.1

WEEK 1	1. 7	WEEK 2	2.10½	WEEK 3	3.10
1. 2	1. 9	2. 1	2.13	3. 3	3.14½
1. 3½	1.11½	2. 4	2.15	3. 5	4. 1½
1. 4½	1.13½	2. 8½	3. 0	3. 6	4. 4

We check the weight of our growing dogs during their first year. In the picture on page 101 you will see a four weeks puppy being weighed. The scale pan has a thick paper towel in it, and the puppy is relaxed and happy at her weekly weigh-in. The picture below shows how to check the weight of a six months bitch puppy before dosing for worms. Stand on the bathroom scales yourself, then stand on them with the puppy in your arms, then subtract your own weight from the combined one – both physical and mental exercise!

A bitch of six months of average size would weigh about 50 lb. The ideal weight for an adult bitch when fully developed and when she is near her twenty-four months is between 60-70 lb, although a well-proportioned animal may weigh several pounds more without giving the impression of being overweight. If the animal is in hard condition with firm muscles, the extra weight can be carried without detracting from either type or utility – it is softness of condition and flabby muscles which are so disfiguring. A dog at six months could easily weigh 60-65 lb, and end up at his full maturity weighing 80 lb. Some animals make their major growth by the time they are six to eight months old, while others may be quite small at this age and then suddenly start to grow. We do not know too well how a dog will finish until the end of the second year. The general appearance depends very much on two things in particular – the proportions and

How to weigh the adult dog on the bathroom scales.

balance of construction, and the hardness of condition. We do not want bulky, clumsy Shepherd Dogs, and above all, we do not want soft-muscled, fleshy ones, so that a few pounds over the desirable and stipulated weight should not be faulted if the balance and firmness are there.

Weight control, as in humans, is done by decreasing the food intake and increasing the exercise, both of which mean strict control of the dog and yourself – no goodies, of course. The dog will not enjoy having his meals cut, so make the reduction gradually. Cut out all rusk or biscuit meal, and slightly increase the raw meat, do not give any additives or vitamin supplements which increase the appetite, and if you fear that he will lose his show 'bloom', put one raw egg yolk on his meat. In very cold weather, if he has been getting a warm drink at bedtime, give him instead a ½ pint of hot water with one teaspoonful of honey and one tablespoonful only of evaporated milk. If he becomes constipated from the lack of his bulk food, give a dessertspoonful of Milk of Magnesia twice weekly in the early morning. He needs a minimum of one hour's exercise and all the freedom, stick throwing and chasing that you can find time for, and a couple of energetic young companions in the exercise pen will work wonders by their teasing and tearing around.

If the dog is too thin, first check for worms and dose carefully if necessary. If you are in any doubt, ask the veterinary surgeon to make a test on the dog's stools, of which you submit a small sample. Here again, the rule is 'no goodies'. Although they can truly be blamed for increasing weight, treats are more likely to spoil his appetite for his correct food and make him dainty, so that he never eats heartily, and this keeps him thin. If he lacks appetite, try a 24-hour fast by giving him a tablespoon of Milk of Magnesia or some rhubarb pills (from the pet shop) in the early mornings, and only small drinks of milk, water and honey at his meal times. The following day, give ½ lb of raw meat at midday, and 1½ lb in the evening. By now he should be hungry, and you can give him a breakfast of semolina porridge, as you did when he was a puppy. Add to it an egg yolk and a dessertspoonful of the old-fashioned weight-builder Virol. Alternatively, put him on a course of Collovet (Crookes), which is obtained from your veterinary surgeon. Until his weight is normal, we recommend giving him two smaller meals – a large one may nauseate him. So at midday he can have 1 lb of cheap white fish, baked in milk in the oven and carefully boned, to which you add a handful of wholemeal rusk or some biscuit, a teaspoonful of olive oil and an egg yolk, and feed when cool. His second meal can be given a little later than his usual main meal, say at 6-7 pm. Ring the changes with raw and cooked meat to stimulate his interest – on one day give 1½ lb of raw horseflesh, on another 1¼ lb of cooked breast of lamb plus ¼ lb of cooked liver, on another 1½ lb of raw or cooked ox heart and on another 1½ lb of raw ox cheek. Mix the chosen meat with a handful of rusk or biscuit and a little gravy, and add a tablespoonful of raw grated suet. A word of caution. Never give cooked and raw meat together in the same meal as the mixture causes stomach upsets. It is also wrong to store cooked and raw meat together in the refrigerator; put them on separate shelves with the cooked meat in a plastic bag or container. Last thing at night, give a small drink of milk, water and honey. He will need his exercise, but curb the romping, and no games with sticks. Particularly after meals, he needs rest.

We have dealt with the various aspects of weight all together, as young adults are usually the 'problem children' where excess or lack of weight are concerned, and it is during the developing stage that the adjustments are most easily made. Bitches vary in weight more than dogs. Many swell in belly just prior to starting a heat, while others improve in condition following the heat period, regardless of whether or not they have been mated. It is all the result of the glandular cycle, and the only way to help them through this is to keep them off all milk and starch, and simply feed one meal of 1½ lb meat with one egg yolk, and give lots of exercise. Within ten days the normal weight should be restored and the soft condition dispelled. In very obstinate cases a teaspoonful of Epsom Salts, dissolved in a little warm water, can be given twice a week during the treatment.

To conclude the questions on weight, do not confuse this with size or maturity. We must not forget that our breed comes to maturity very slowly, and that a young dog can appear, by comparison, to be underweight if seen beside a dog which is fully matured. In actual fact, the young dog may be exactly right for his age and phase of development. If German Shepherds are slow to attain their full growth, we are compensated by their lasting qualities, as many of our dogs are at their best around five to six years, when some other breeds are already retired. Bone, too, has to strengthen and smooth down as the dog goes through adolescence. Our puppies have knobbly knees like any schoolboy, and this is sometimes thought to be rickets when in truth it merely indicates that the dog will be of good size. In any case, a puppy fed as we have recommended is extremely unlikely to be suffering from a disease of deficiency, such as rickets, the indications of which are soft, easily dislocated or broken bones.

When writing of development one could just as easily write 'wait' for 'weight', because as you will have realized the exact future of even the best-looking puppy is very much in the air. We can only feed him, give full attention, fresh air and exercise and hope that by our careful upbringing, suited to the needs of the Shepherd Dog, we can combat the results of close in-breeding, lack of freedom, and sometimes even of city life, where many of our working dogs must, perforce, lead their lives. 'Back to nature' should be our aim in every way possible, giving the growing animal every opportunity to use his exceptional gifts. Only kennel a Shepherd when it is absolutely necessary. Four walls and a small, caged enclosure twenty-four hours a day are the certain death of all the things which spell German Shepherd Dog – lively character, firm, well-muscled limbs and a confident way of meeting life instead of shying away from it.

11 All About Socialization of the Puppy

We have dwelt at some length on the physical needs of the growing dog and, of course, this is highly important. Some very intellectual people have puny bodies, but with our dog his brawn must match his brain or he is not typical. I am not for a moment suggesting that only physically perfect dogs should be allowed to live, as some animals carry very desirable characteristics along with a few faults. It really depends on how far these faults are hereditary, or known to be carried in that particular line. If they are mental faults, then you should, in justice to the dog, yourself and the breed, not proceed with such blood-lines.

Puppy quietly accepting his daily handling session.

Any experienced breeder will tell you how frequently trouble comes along when dealing with livestock, without courting it by knowingly introducing unsoundness.

There are several books written by knowledgeable and experienced people about temperament, behaviour, dog-human relationships and kindred topics. They can be read and supply many useful ideas about dogs and their conduct, and personally I enjoy them all, as people whose business is noting the reaction of dogs in our highly civilized world always fascinate me. However, we are really concerned with the German Shepherd Dog, and the notes which follow are mostly concerned with him. All dogs have much in common, but our dog *is* different in many ways. He is bred to be a dog of service – how else could he have risen to the height of popularity he enjoys today in all branches of canine service? That he is also the family dog par excellence shows the depth of his character and his great adaptability. We must all do our best to keep him on his pinnacle, and understanding his early reactions to life will help us to do so, I am sure you will agree.

When the newly-born puppies lie beside their mother, mostly sleeping or jostling for the best 'bottles' at the bar, one could say that nothing registers with them or affects their future outlook. I am not sure that they are completely insensitive even at eight days old. Being a dyed-in-the-wool baby worshipper, I handle them and talk to them from the start, and it is always a great joy when their eyes open (during their second week, normally) and little heads lift or turn towards me as I enter their kennel and they hear my voice. A strange voice heard at two to three weeks will often cause a puppy to 'freeze' and remain quite still, which I have always thought to be a return to the reaction of nestlings in the long years ago when they cowered silently in their lair if strangers approached. By the time the puppies are three weeks old they start their family relationship, and will make wild swipes at each other (they cannot focus properly at this age) and grab each other's ears in mock battle. They will also show interest, and even affection, by licking the breeder's hand or cheek if held close.

If you have hand-weaned them onto meat as we have suggested you will have had plenty of individual contact with the litter, but if you rear your puppies by a less personal method, do, I beg of you, handle them all two or three times per day. This handling is the true basis of the puppy's future education. It is his 'play school', where his confidence in human beings begins, just as a four year old child begins to feel a warm relationship with his teacher based on friendly confidence. He will also start to learn respect for other dogs, as his mother will be drying up soon and will be teaching the puppies when and where they may have a quick stand-up drink/snack . . . and when *not*! If you have another older, good-natured dog or bitch and the mother raises no objections, you can allow it in with the litter, or put them all outside together if the weather is dry and not too cold. All my own dogs are brought up together, and I think they bring each other up. When a bitch is in labour, the other bitches – even maidens – cry and are upset; and the stud dogs make wonderful 'uncles', and will play ridiculous games with five or six weeks old puppies and allow some very undignified assaults on their persons. Dogs recognize their own close relations, too. If we have to bring a new dog into the kennel at any time, it is much easier to get it accepted if it is related to my own stock. This would seem to be engendered by their 'family' upbringing and teaching.

But – you should not leave older dogs with puppies or youngsters unless you are there to supervize them. I know of several occasions when a puppy, or small dog, has been left with two older or larger ones. The puppy annoys one adult and is dealt a correction, it screams in protest, the second adult thinks it should also teach it a lesson and soon the poor puppy is mauled and will not be likely to survive such treatment. The dogs are not to blame. It is our responsibility to see that such chances are not taken, for although we love them dearly dogs are animals and their instinctive reactions are animal ones. No training can alter this fact, and it must be borne in mind always. You can get a near-human relationship between dog and human who work in close co-operation, you can get two dogs to work (together) under human influence, but with more than two dogs you are bound, sooner or later, to get a 'pack' reaction, and this can be dangerous. All this may seem a long way ahead of the two to three weeks old puppy we are discussing, yet these lessons begin at that age, and it is interesting to see how they influence the dog later in life.

During the next two weeks the puppy will be growing curious and inquisitive, and the little rascal will escape from his box, climb out of his kennel door and investigate the great world outside. His mother will be his 'pack leader' at this stage, so watch how the puppy reacts when she barks. If she sounds an alarm, he will scuttle back to bed or run to his mother's side. If the mother is friendly and forthcoming it is a wonderful help to the puppies' outlook on life, for they will run forward to greet visitors and boldly bark at the birds which invade their run, in imitation of their mother. However, if her temperament is nervous or suspect, keep her away from the litter when you are giving them an airing or introducing them to 'fields fresh and pastures new'. They will learn better from your quiet chatter, gentle handling and presentation of new things than they will from the unreliable reactions of the mother, who can ruin their confidence at this early stage if she is herself nervous.

An alert and confident well-socialized fourteen-week old dog puppy.

Alert, attentive and willing nine weeks old bitch puppy.

From six weeks onwards, the puppy will begin to follow you around, he will start to become attentive when called (I don't mean when he sees his dinner bowl), he will 'claim' you when you squat down in the kennel to fuss the litter and growl at his litter-mates who will also claim you and growl at *him*. He is becoming a personality and is bent on establishing himself as an individual. This progress makes some people think that six weeks is the ideal time to separate the puppy and send it out to its new owner. I am afraid I do not agree. Puppies need each other to play with, to curl up against and sleep with, to stimulate appetite by competition at the feeding bowl and to maintain at this sensitive period (teething and growing fast) the comforts of their familiar life. They will by now be separated from their mother almost entirely, and will usually form attachments among themselves; we often notice the same two babies cuddling up together – invariably two of the same colour, too. We like to keep our litter intact until it is nine weeks old. The puppy which leaves at this age is sturdy, is becoming independent and, above all, is now completely separated from the mother and is ready to accept a human leader and 'litter-mate' – someone to teach him games which have the basis of training (he is a Shepherd Dog, and expects to be trained) and to establish the dog-master link at its most appropriate time. The puppy is more receptive now than at any other time in its life, both to its owner/trainer and to its environment. Thus, we feel that our puppies are better equipped to face their new life at this age, and that we have made it easier for them by keeping them with us for the extra few weeks.

Once the puppy is away from his breeder and in good hands he will quickly develop as an individual, and enjoy his self-importance in his new surroundings. While we have had many touching reunions with our own puppies long after they have left us, we know that, with mercifully few exceptions, most of them do not miss us once they have settled with kind new owners, and that they are delighted to be the centre of attraction and attention. We like to think that we have equipped them to this end, and that their start in life has given them the right slant on human beings and confidence for their future.

12 All About Grooming

The young dog does not really need grooming as an adult does, with his deep, thick coat. However, we like to make twofold use of the grooming interlude, so we put our nine weeks old puppies onto the big, old wooden table (a bench will do equally well) where all our dogs are brushed, and passing a hand underneath them we encourage them to stretch out into a show stance, having made sure they are standing well-balanced, with the front feet directly under the shoulders in an easy position. Soothe the puppy with the hand and the voice, 'Good, Bero', and 'Stand, Bero', until after a few lessons he is accustomed to stand still while you examine him. Then run your hand down his back and give him the command 'Bero, sit!', pressing on his hind-quarters meanwhile. When he is sitting quietly, tilt his muzzle up so that you can see his dentition, gently lifting the front lips to display the 'bite' (where the upper and lower front teeth meet) and then lifting the side lips left and right to display the premolars and aftermolars. Reassure him constantly, and when the examination is completed feed him a goody and praise him warmly. It is worth spending time to get Bero to co-operate in having his teeth examined, as this will be a great help if he is to have a show career. Many dogs refuse outright to let the judge see the teeth, and others struggle violently and waste everyone's time in the ring. But, we repeat, if he is gently handled *and* rewarded, it is unlikely that Bero will resent opening his mouth. Even if you have no intention of exhibiting Bero, it is a sound idea to get him accustomed to mouth examination in case he is ill at any time and requires attention from the veterinary surgeon for his throat or mouth.

Now you should take a look at his ears, which should be free from spots or redness and cool to the touch. If there is any sign of tenderness, look right down inside for any evidence of canker (ear mites). This is a painful affliction, and gives off a thick, reddish-brown discharge with an unpleasant, mouldy odour. It develops quickly to spread all through the many channels and crevices of the dog's ears, and is not easily cured unless caught in the early stages. Should you detect this horrid odour, or have suspicions that canker has started, wrap a cleansing tissue around your index finger, and gently wipe round as deep as possible, and if you find the dark discharge, ask your veterinary surgeon to confirm the infection and prescribe treatment. There are many 'canker cures' on sale at chemists and pet shops, but we always feel that ears are as precious as eyes to the dog, and should have professional care when infected. *Never* pour anything liquid into the ears unless so advised professionally, as it could cause intense pain and great damage. The ears should be gently cleaned once weekly by wrapping a tissue round your finger and gently loosening dirt and wax. Puppies get very dirty ears from digging vigorously so that the earth flies into them, and this will set up irritation unless removed promptly. A piece of old linen, soaked in sweet almond oil, will loosen any dry or stubborn dirt and will not cause grass or similar seeds to swell and aggravate the trouble.

The teeth do not normally require cleaning until well into the second year. If there are any stains on the enamel, or the teeth are dingy in colour following gastric disturbance, dip a piece of old linen in peroxide of hydrogen (10 vol) and then into powdered pumice (obtained from your chemist) and rub the stain very gently so as not to hurt the tender gums. Rinse well with clean water afterwards.

Bero's nose may be dry or cracked, again possibly as the result of digging, or in cold weather of rooting in snow. Carefully smoothe a little white vaseline into the sore places.

Now the eyes claim our attention. If they have been running or have mucous in the corners, he could have a grass seed in there under a lid, or if you take him to the beach for exercise the fine sand may have irritated them. Bathe thoroughly and sympathetically with cool boiled water in which you have put two large pinches of boric acid, sometimes called boracic. A few drops of the human eye remedy 'Murine' is very soothing, and you can keep the tube of veterinary antibiotic eye ointment handy, putting a small quantity in each corner of the eye if the soreness persists.

Next for our inspection are the feet. Look between the pads for any thorns or cuts, look at the pads themselves to see if there are any cuts or torn nails, which can cause lameness. Any such troubles should be bathed with cool water containing a few drops of T.C.P. or similar disinfectant, and after drying carefully, some antibiotic powder (obtainable from your veterinary surgeon) should be dusted into the wounds. We keep a 'puffer' bottle of this powder on our grooming tray as 'instant first-aid', and find it invaluable for treating minor tears and cuts.

Lift up the tail to see if there are any segments of tapeworm sticking to the fur, and also to see if there is any soreness of the anus which may indicate trouble with the anal glands, a condition from which our breed suffers frequently, according to the veterinary profession. A dog with this trouble will constantly drag his behind along the floor, as the condition is very uncomfortable and even painful. It is best prevented by feeding a correct diet with plenty of roughage as we recommend.

Soft foods allow the anal gland to fill with a yellowish fluid, whereas bulky foods press them clean in the moment of elimination. Treatment is best left to your veterinary surgeon. If you have to clean the glands yourself, cover your palm with a fairly thick layer of cottonwool and place it across the anus, feel for the glands (they are like little lumps under the skin) with the thumb and finger, and squeeze them to force the fluid into the cottonwool which should be disposed of immediately by burning. You should also inspect your bitches for any sign of the vulva swelling, which shows that she is preparing to come on heat – you may want to arrange in good time for her to go into 'purdah'. You can press a cleansing tissue on her vulva for evidence of any 'colour' or stain.

Everyone has a favourite way of cleaning the coat. Rittmeister von Stephanitz did not approve of combs, and advised spare use of the brush. He considered that combs tear out the undercoat, and break the top coat and guard hairs, and he preferred hound gloves and a fairly soft brush to work right through the coat. It is true to say that excessive combing and brushing at the moulting period can break the new hairs and slow up the re-growth of the coat. If the dog leads a fairly or completely natural life, with access to rough grassland and hedges, he will roll ecstatically in the grass at moulting time and remove a lot of hair in this way, and also by running through hedges and bushes. Our own method, if we want to get the old coat out quickly, is to bath the dog and remove the loose hair when he is wet, using the hands and a chamois leather. We like whalebone or dandy brushes, as used for ponies, as we find that nylon breaks the hair. The comb should be fairly wide-toothed and heavy, so that it passes easily through the thick coat without tearing the hair.

The ordinary, everyday brushing which follows the physical inspection starts with running the comb backwards through the coat, to make sure that no 'inhabitants' have taken up residence overnight; one flea can quickly populate the entire kennel and give you endless work to be rid of them. A reliable brand of flea powder should form part of your grooming kit. Cover the dog's head with a piece of clean cloth while you sprinkle the powder around the ruff, or you may start sore eyes or even respiratory trouble if the powerful stuff gets into eyes or nose. Now use your brush, and groom quite hard in a rotary action to stimulate the hair and clean it. Then settle it down in the right direction with short brush strokes. Don't overlook the head and underneath parts, or the legs, but use a softer brush here. You can put a final polish on the coat with a chamois leather or one of the many kinds of hound gloves. Finally, take note of any bare patches on the elbows, where you should rub in a little of a home-made remedy consisting of equal quantities of white vaseline and coconut oil mixed and melted together. This will keep the skin soft, and will help the hair to grow again. Take care that the dog does not lick any of the salve, as it will make him very sick.

The nails need care, too, and if the dog is exercised mostly on grass, they may not keep as short as required. It is best, of course, to wear them down with walking on hard roads or pavements. If it is found necessary to trim them, do this with the utmost care; you will need a helper, as very few dogs are co-operative in this matter. It is better to cut very little at a time, and when you see the spongy 'quick' appear you will know it is time to stop. Use only the correct type of nail clippers designed for canine use. If you have the misfortune to cut the soft tissue and make the nail bleed, dab with iodine immediately. The dog may be footsore for some time, so do not trim the nails any time near a show date.

One of those plastic trays which are sold for storing cutlery in drawers is ideal for use as a grooming tray, and you can keep all your equipment together tidily and ready to hand. If there is a handyman around, a light wooden tray could be made up quite easily. Transfer all ointments etc. into plastic, unbreakable containers, as a restless dog could overturn the tray and injure himself or you by broken glass if this is not done. The grooming brushes should be washed each week, and a few drops of some pleasant-smelling disinfectant should be sprinkled on the bristles after the final rinsing, to keep them smelling fresh. We give here a list of useful items for your tray:

Brushes, comb, grooming glove or washleather, cottonwool, cleansing tissues, elbow salve, flea powder, mild disinfectant, iodine, eye-lotion or ointment, nail clippers, forceps to pull thorns or ticks, small plastic bag (to hold hair-combings) and puffer bottle of Aureomycin powder (antibiotic).

We now come to the vexed question of bathing. Most dogs have as much liking for soap and hot water as the average small boy! However, a dog which lives in a town or lies about the house needs regular bathing – about every six or eight weeks should suffice. A dog which is bedded on soft compressed pine shavings (wood-wool) will seldom require bathing, as this type of bedding not only cleans the coat but discourages fleas etc. It is ideal for small puppies, as it has a cosy quality. Unfortunately, it is not suitable for bedding 'house' dogs, as it is untidy stuff and flies everywhere.

In winter or cool weather, the dog must be bathed indoors – in the human's bath tub. Only in really warm weather can he be bathed out-of-doors.

Collect together everything you may possibly need, as once the dog is in the bath you will not be able to leave him for an instant. Ask your veterinary surgeon for a good and suitable shampoo, or obtain one from the pet shop. Johnson's Baby Shampoo is recommended for puppies. Comb all the loose hairs out before he enters the bathroom. Have ready two or three towels (warm, if possible) and large washleather. Smear a trace of white vaseline round the rim of the eyes, or some golden eye ointment if you prefer, to prevent the shampoo from making the eyes smart. You can lightly plug the ears with cottonwool, too. This helps to prevent him from fidgeting if water should splash into the ears. One of the rubber handshower sprays which fits over the taps is excellent for rinsing purposes – it really removes the soap. However, a watering can with a fine rose will do the job well, but with rather more trouble, as it also requires a helper to pour the water while you control the dog. A large waterproof apron will protect you from a soaking.

Make sure that the water is not too hot – 98°-100°F is warm enough. Stand your dog in three or four inches of water and wet him all over with the hands or pouring from a plastic cup. Next apply the shampoo, and working from the tail forwards rub it well into the coat and under the legs until you reach the ruff. Do not on any account use soap on the head, but wipe over with the leather or a piece of old towelling, wrung out in hot water, or a sponge. Soap and rinse twice, making quite sure that all the shampoo has been removed. You can pour a jug of warm water with three or four tablespoonsful of vinegar in it to make a final, effective rinse, if you wish it. Throw a big towel right over the dog before he is lifted out of the bath, or he will soak you from the vigorous shaking he performs as soon as he is free. He will remove more water in two good shakings than you can do with half a dozen towels. Dry him as speedily as possible as dogs are prone to chills – far more so than human beings, actually. The washleather, well wrung out in clean hot water, will remove the moisture easily, and a brisk towelling and, if possible, a session under a portable electric hair-dryer, will soon have him comfortable and out of danger. He can lie on clean newspaper to blot off any remaining dampness on a cold day. In warm weather a brisk run will be helpful, but watch that he does not roll in the dust (or worse!), which is something dogs love to do when they have been bathed. You will by now have wiped off the ointment from around his eyes and removed the ear plugs. As soon as he is reasonably dry, comb the hair back into position, and brush when quite dry. If you fear that he may have become chilled for any reason while being bathed, give him a warm drink of milk, water and honey.

If weather conditions are suitable for the bath to be given out-of-doors, the procedure is really the same, with perhaps minor modifications. For example, it may be possible to rig a hose through the kitchen window for the rinsing stage, as an alternative to the watering can, and if the weather is *really* hot, a swimsuit is certainly the most sensible garb for yourself. But whatever the circumstances, be sure to talk reassuringly to your dog all through the ordeal, and try to persuade him that all this special fuss is for his benefit. Some dogs actually enjoy this extra attention, although we are bound to admit that the majority submit only under vigorous protest, or at best suffer it most unwillingly.

13 All About Exercise

We have mentioned the importance of proper exercise many times already, but the type of exercise may well depend on the area where the dog lives, and on his owner's way of life, which naturally has much to do, one way and another, with deciding what is possible. Our dog's first requirement is some freedom, a place where he can run, jump, sniff and potter around. A piece of rough ground, fenced in, or a small orchard is excellent if available, and ten minutes of stick throwing or romping with a canine companion will do as much for his back and thigh muscles as an hour on the road. Put up a jump or two when he is old enough, and if you have a child Shepherd enthusiast, hide and seek is a favourite game. We have a bitch who 'owns' two schoolboys, and they have taught her to keep goal so well that to date nobody has scored!

Road work is essential for achieving and maintaining the much prized well-knuckled toes and short nails. It also teaches discipline, and a good mile each day should be the minimum. In the country areas of Germany, and also in Switzerland and Austria, one often sees a dog trotting beside a bicycle being ridden at a slow pace. This is very good

Freedom to romp is a 'must' for healthy firm-muscled Shepherd Dogs.

indeed, *if* one can find a place where it is safe to cycle, but it is even more difficult, perhaps, to find one where it is also safe to have a dog trotting alongside. If you have a quarry or a gravel pit in the neighbourhood where it is safe to enter, these make ideal places for exercise both for feet and backs; climbing steep banks is wonderful for developing shoulders, too.

All exercise should be worked up to gradually, for the same reasons that humans must not suddenly indulge in violent exercise. It is a strain on the animal if he has to lie about all the week, and then goes on a ten mile hike at the week-end. One realizes that in many cases the week-end is the only opportunity for a long walk, but *some* exercise should be fitted in every day, wet or fine, early or late, if the dog is to be kept in a proper, hard condition.

Swimming is fine for the shoulders and back muscles, if less good for the coat condition. We have a long line of 'water babies' in our kennel, and I have yet to hear of a German Shepherd which did not enjoy swimming and playing in the water. One new owner, at least, has telephoned to complain that the puppy insisted on diving into the goldfish pond or water-lily pool! So take your dog swimming in all but the coldest weather. Let him shake well, and give him a rough towelling when he reaches home. Swimming does not seem to wet the undercoat, and a dog dries much quicker after swimming than after a bath, when the soapy water has been rubbed into the undercoat.

For the show dog, brisk walking is by far the best, of course. Following a rider on bicycle or horse, even ridden slowly, seems to extend the trot and make it impossible for even the most agile handler to keep pace with the dog in the ring. An 'only' dog is more difficult to keep fit than one which has a companion to romp with and keep him on his toes.

Whilst it is recognized that many dogs must live in cities, to do their work as police and guard dogs, we hope that care is taken to allow them some freedom between their spells of duty, and we hope that nobody who has a warm regard for the breed will ever take one to live in the town for their own personal pleasure. The restrictions of a town environment are all against the breed's proper development and normal way of life.

As most people know, a dog should not be exercised after his main meal but rather before it, as running about with a full stomach places a great strain on both back and muscles and can result in lifelong digestive trouble. We have to remember that when a dog has had his main exercise and his main meal he is not 'finished' for the day. When he has rested and digested a bit he will be eager to play or join with his 'family' in some recreation. Otherwise, if he is shut up, or left to his own devices, he will get into mischief, chew up your possessions (only the best, naturally!) and even bark noisily out of sheer boredom. He needs an outlet in some form of training, or a romp and some game with children or his owner. In short, when you take on a German Shepherd, you take on some work, too. If you want to get full enjoyment from this remarkable animal, you must give him all the time and companionship you can manage. Then you will have a healthy, contented animal who will reward you wholeheartedly with his courageous, endearing nature and astonishing intelligence.

14 All About Showing a German Shepherd Dog

Exhibiting beautiful dogs in immaculate condition, well-schooled in ringcraft and skilfully presented, is a pleasure, a hobby and a sport in any breed, and one which absorbs and thrills an enormous number of dedicated people. We do not want to go into all the aspects of showing, which are at least as many as those of dog breeding, only mentioning that the social side is perhaps the most compelling. A dog show is a splendid opportunity to get to know others who share your interest, and to gain knowledge of the breed (*and* of humans). It is a feast for the eyes, too – and we do not mean that you should feast your eyes just on the prize winners. Judges' opinions vary considerably and you can gain your own experience, and amusement, in making your own choice for the placings. One has to remember, however, that Lady Luck is at her most fickle at dog shows. So be prepared for lots of ups and downs, don't spoil the fun with a too serious outlook and never expect that it will bring any financial reward, as this is surely the most unlikely thing to happen.

We are fortunate in owning a naturally presented breed – that is, one which does not require hours of preparation and trimming by experts, as is the case with such as the Poodle, Terrier or Afghan. It has the disadvantage, though, of not possessing a thick, long coat to cloak its faults or enhance its beauty, and no clever trimming can ever help to fool the eye. All that the dog has, or has not, is there for all to see, and the discerning eye is not distracted by show preparation. This is one reason why so much attention must be paid to the daily care of the dog, and to giving him sufficient exercise and freedom to keep him in hard, sound condition, so that he makes a good impression of a working dog in the ring.

To school a dog for show presentation may take hours of very real effort, in which concentration plays a great part; one has only to watch the top handlers to realize that they never relax their hold over the exhibit. Some even appear to mesmerize them, so intent do they keep the dogs. If you can afford to engage a professional handler it will simplify matters. If one is no longer young, or not in the very good physical condition needed to keep up with the long periods of fast 'gaiting', then a handler is almost a 'must', but it adds considerably to the already heavy expense of showing a dog. These people frequently like to take the dog into their own kennels for a period, to assess him and find the best way of presenting him to his advantage, and as the best ones fill their engagement diaries early, it is important to approach them in good time.

If you are going to handle your dog yourself, which is really much more fun, then you should join a local training society which holds ringcraft classes, so that your dog becomes accustomed to moving round the ring in company with others and to being touched, particularly around the mouth, by strangers. These societies hold matches, where you can gain experience far beyond that which pages of written advice can give you. Approach the experienced breeders and ask for guidance. Most of our breeders are friendly and will help to put a newcomer on the right lines, whatever their attitude when you start to collect the prizes! You must also give yourself a course of training, always entering the ring calm and relaxed, as any tension you may feel will travel straight down the lead to your dog, and make him as fussy and jumpy as yourself! We have seen a dog faulted for bad nerves behaving perfectly in the hands of a quiet and confident handler at a later show.

Now, about your own part in preparing the dog for the show. As the event is advertised several weeks ahead of the date, and as Championship Shows publish their dates at the beginning of the year, you will have plenty of time to condition your dog. Some extra road work is advisable, to make sure his feet are in good 'working' order and to correct any overweight or soft condition which can have come on during winter or bad weather restrictions. Give him a tablespoonful of suet (freshly grated) on his main meal, to help his coat condition, and work on it with a couple of firmly bristled brushes, to cleanse it and make it gleam. The brushes can be washed and dried after each use to give the dog an immaculate look, even when bathing is not possible for weather or other reasons. Always make sure grooming tools are kept spotlessly clean.

In a breed with an erect ear carriage dirt is most noticeable, so clean the ears gently with a tissue and a few drops of sweet almond oil, which will loosen any hard matter. Put a small plug of cottonwool in the ear first, so that none can trickle inside to irritate him and cause disastrous scratching. You can obtain ear-cleaning products at the pet shop if preferred. Do remember to remove the ear plugs when all is finished. We discussed nail trimming in the chapter on grooming. If this attention should be necessary, do it at least a week before the show date, so that if you have the misfortune to cut or tear a nail it will then have time to heal. Check his mouth for tartar or stains on the teeth, and start to remove these with a piece of old soft linen dipped in Peroxide (10 vol) and then in powdered pumice, which must be well rinsed out afterwards.

Bitches at the Ring-side

Above: 'Look! Here she comes, all "spit and polish" – hair spray, I've heard some say.'

Centre: 'All that manoeuvring and still she looks like you know what.'

Below: 'My dear, just look at those feet and pasterns!'

Above: 'Of course, she'll win. Just between ourselves, I once saw the judge patting her grandmother.'

Below: 'Ha! Ha! Just as I said – it's really just a big fiddle.'

It is all a matter of luck whether your dog is in coat or in moult. If the former, then you will only need the extra cleansing with brushes to produce a gleaming coat; if the latter, do comb and brush out all loose hairs and tufts, which only accentuate his shedding coat condition. Naturally, all judges prefer a full coat, but many do not penalize heavily for lack of it if the dog is in hard condition and of clean appearance. Inspect his 'pants' and comb them thoroughly to remove any dirt or excreta that may be adhering. Most of these attentions will have been given daily if you have read the chapter on grooming; all that remains is for you to check on all points and give a final polish with a soft washleather on the great day. It helps one's confidence in the ring to know that one has a spotless, hard-conditioned dog which cannot be faulted on that account, whatever his shortcomings may be otherwise.

In these enlightened days all show dogs and the majority of pets are inoculated against the dreaded killer diseases, which has removed a great load of anxiety from the breeders' minds. We are thus not so much concerned, in this country anyway, with health precautions as we were before the advent of antibiotics. However, we still like to swab out the mouths of our show-goers with cottonwool dipped in T.C.P. or some suitable mouth disinfectant both *before* and after the show. An old towel, soaked in strong disinfectant and kept ready in a plastic bag, can be spread on the garage floor for you to sterilize your shoes and the returning dogs their feet. This is especially important if you have un-inoculated puppies in the nest. It is better to keep the show dogs well away from the puppy house for forty-eight hours, and to take their temperatures night and morning for the same period if you have seen, or heard of, any sickness at the show, and at the first sign of any trouble, get your veterinary surgeon to come immediately. Some kinds of enteritis can be picked up at shows, where occasionally sick dogs are carelessly allowed to soil the ground. Unless treatment is given at once the infection can spread all through your kennel, and it may take you some weeks to get normal health restored.

Ringcraft and presentation are better learned from example than from the written word. However, for the sake of those who are not near enough to a training club, or for any reason cannot attend one, we will take you through the method of presenting the dog. The German breeders have a manner of presentation which shows the Shepherd Dog naturally and to his advantage. The dogs are taught to move ahead of the handler on the full length of a lead quite twice the length of our normal ones. This free striding gives them an attractive alertness and enhances the natural head carriage with an air of independent spirit and fearless expression which seems to say: 'Look! I've out-manoeuvred everyone and can do this all by myself!' This is our Shepherd Dog at his best, and to see a large ringful, of some hundred dogs, all moving like this at the Hauptzuchtschau is a thrill for all devotees of the breed. Unfortunately, in this country we rarely have a ring large enough for our well-filled classes to move properly. Outdoor venues seldom seem to mark out sufficient space for us, while most indoor rings are small and frustrating for both judge and exhibitors. However, we must learn to handle our dogs within these limits, and take advantage of the clear run round the ring at their individual examination to display their gait, which can be restricted in the collective running round if the ring is overcrowded.

Do not make the mistake of over-handling and manoeuvring your exhibit, and, above all, never 'string him up' on a tight lead (like a Boxer or other breed with an arched neck). This 'stringing up' may give an alert appearance by raising the head, but it spoils the balance and creates a straight line down through the shoulder as the dog is prevented from putting his weight normally on his two front feet, which place the shoulder in normal position. Then, with the greater part of his weight forced back onto his hind legs, he sinks down in hind-quarters to assume an ugly, crouching position which is often mistaken for 'good hind angulation', and which quickly disappears once the dog's head is released or when he moves, unless he is very nervous and therefore gaits in this untypical crouching manner through fear. Speaking from the judge's point of view, one's worst suspicions are aroused by any kind of 'circus tricks' or any show of 'clever' positioning of a dog, as it is done more often than not to cover up faults and to endeavour to fool the judge. So try to walk your dog into a natural stance, and when you have taught him to hold the position in which you think he looks his best (this takes quite a number of lessons), step back the length of his lead so that he is standing alone and can be viewed easily by the judge.

Enlist the help of a friend or another breeder or exhibitor for whom you can render the same service. Ask the helper to act as judge and show him the dog's mouth. If you have taught your puppy from his early days to accept having his jaws opened at grooming time, you may have no difficulty in displaying his dentition to the judge. One of the safest ways is to sit your dog and straddle his back with your knees either side to control him while you use your hands on his head. Tilt his nose upwards by placing one hand under his chin, and with the other part his front lips to show the 'bite' (the front top teeth resting on the lower ones and even overlapping them slightly). Most judges only wish to see that the desired 'scissor bite' is present in a puppy, since the premolars and aftermolars may not yet all be through the gums. If your dog is out of the puppy classes, then you must also lift each side of the lip in turn so that the molars and canines can be examined. Try to keep your own head behind the dog's – so many exhibitors seem to get between the judge and the dog in their efforts to look in the mouth themselves!

Now you must pose your dog, or 'stand' or 'set him up' which are expressions used in the ring. Some judges like to see the dog posed and to take their notes before looking at the mouth. You can ask, without entering into a conversation, what you are to do first. Stand him naturally, with his front feet set naturally apart and straight, while one hind leg should be positioned forward and slightly under the body in the classic stance. The way to achieve this varies with the way the dog responds to the handler. He may allow his limbs to be moved into position and stand 'statue-still' during his examination, or he may be curious or lively and fidget after a minute, so that you have to move him in a circle back into position again for the judge to complete his assessment. Don't worry if this happens as the judge is accustomed to it, and he (or she) has come to see the dog and is prepared to wait a little for him to settle. Now the judge may run his hands over the dog, testing the firmness of the back and the spring of the ribs. He may also wish to test him for 'entirety', and your helper must go about this sensitive business very carefully so that the dog is not startled or hurt, as the testicles are his most tender and vulnerable parts – which may make this a difficult task. If one hand is run gently down the dog's back, ending with a pat on the rump and a reassuring word to the dog, the other can discreetly explore the scrotum to establish that both testicles are descended properly. You should hold his slip collar very firmly just now, as if he is accidentally hurt he may turn on his examiner in his pain. When this business has been successfully rehearsed a few times, the dog usually accepts it without fuss, unless a careless or hurried gesture hurts him. Always, therefore, be on your guard at this point of the examination, in case of some reaction.

A tit-bit secreted in the hand is often used to keep the dog interested and alert in the ring, and while this is an excellent (and permitted) help for the handler it must be emphasized that the goody should never be held above the normal line of the dog's vision. If it is held higher, then the dog will elevate his gaze and even crane forward to reach the food, so that the shoulder line may be straightened and thrown out and the whole of the dog's balance thrown out of true. Remember that you are showing a German Shepherd Dog, which is a forward reaching animal with the head so carried that the chin is on a line with the base of the neck, particularly when in action. So do not fall into the habit of checking your dog so that his head is jerked upwards. He can be taught to move freely the length of his lead ahead of the handler and yet not to pull on the lead. If the dog is sulky or inattentive in the ring, he can sometimes be enlivened by the well-known method of feeding him early on the day previous to the show, and from then on giving him nothing but liquids until he has been in the ring. He will thus be hungry and keen for the tit-bit, and his intelligence will soon prompt him that food follows the show, and it should keep him on his toes. Do not, however, withhold liquids. This is cruel, and also makes him look light and drawn-up in loin, and the underline suffers.

When the examination is completed, you will be asked to move your dog up and down the ring or diagonally from corner to corner in a straight line so that the judge can assess the firmness of limbs and the sequence of steps. This should be done at walking pace for a true revelation of the movement. In any case, whether walking or trotting the dog, do not move him sideways across the ring, since this is a recognized manoeuvre for the 'clever' handler seeking to disguise a weaving or soft action, and may arouse the judge's suspicions even if you are too new to the game to realize it. Next you will have to make a complete circuit of the ring with your dog on the lead on your left side. Don't let your own nerves cause you to hurry or fluster at this point; it is your big moment 'solo' in the ring, and you must make full use of it for your dog's sake. The dog looks at his best if he strides out ahead of you *without* pulling on the lead, as we have already said. So give him a loose lead and let him set the pace, which you must keep up with – or find someone else to run him for you.

After all the dogs in the class have been individually assessed the judge will want to run them round the ring together, and this is where the lessons of your training class will prove to have helped you. The dog must move freely by your side and never ahead of you so that he hinders or obscures the one in front, nor lagging behind to upset or restrict the one following. It is poor sportsmanship to hamper another's chances and you can also ask the handler ahead or behind you to check his dog if it is allowed to interfere with your own. Some judges ask their ring stewards to call in the numbers they are considering for prizes, and then move these around again after those not called have left the ring. If you are placed, thank the steward for your card and keep in position until your number has been noted. Congratulate the owners of any dogs placed over yours, or, if you are in first place say a kind word to the one behind, such as 'I am in luck today', or 'I didn't expect to beat your nice dog today.' It is worth while cultivating a reputation for being a pleasant owner, and jealousy is quite ridiculous when one realizes the tremendous number of things that can go wrong in dog breeding and how precious the occasional and usually well-deserved strokes of good luck are to the hardworking breeder.

If you have entered in a later class, stay near the ring, and if you have already been 'placed' the steward will tell you where to stand when the new class is ready for the final gaiting and the call goes out for 'Old dogs, please!' – old dogs being those shown in any previous class. Be attentive, and don't keep the class waiting while other dogs get restless or bored.

Now a few hints about your dog's and your own comfort at the show. A large, serviceable holdall which can be pushed under your bench is useful to take along your requirements. We will list the usual ones and you can add your personal needs:

Entry passes and car park label (if issued), drinking bowl, grooming kit, towel, small first-aid kit (containing miniature flask of brandy, small-size bottle of disinfectant, cottonwool and tissues, and aspirins), pair of loose cotton gloves, baked liver cubes (or other tit-bit for the ring), meat (in a plastic bag) or a tin of meat – remember the opener! – to give your dog a snack before leaving the show if you will be arriving home long after the usual feeding time, as a cold and hungry dog is susceptible to illness, and a roll of two or three thick newspapers secured with a rubber band, to spread on the bench for warmth and comfort.

Take no bones or toys in case your dog has possessive or jealous reactions to passers-by or visitors to the bench, but bring a large flask of tea or coffee and some substantial easy-to-eat food for yourself, as the food at shows is expensive and not always appetising or easy to obtain without queueing. Besides, you may not want to leave your dog unattended for long, and if you have kennel business there may be enquiries for you to answer when callers approach your bench wanting puppies or stud cards.

15   All About Travelling

Most of us like to take our dog with us when we travel by car, and if you are attending the shows you are most likely to be using your car for transport. Sad to say, many puppies suffer from travel sickness and while the majority adjust themselves to the motion of the vehicle, there are a few which never travel comfortably. So it takes time and patience to effect a cure or to discover if one has a hopeless traveller.

One of the chief causes of vomiting is transporting the dog on the luxuriously sprung rear seat of the modern car. The spring rate of the upholstery is adjusted for the weight of the average adult person, and a puppy (or even an adult dog) is bounced up and down like a tennis ball on the sloping angle of the seat, which makes an uncomfortable bed. An estate car is, therefore, ideal for transporting dogs, and a comfortable and waterproof floor-covering can be made by enclosing a thin mattress or an old sleeping-bag in a plastic cover with a zip fastener. For puppies, it is wise to put down thick newspaper in addition; it makes for easy cleaning and disposal of any car sickness. If yours is a saloon car, you can remove the back seat squab and replace it with an old mattress such as already suggested. If your dogs will be travelling in the car frequently or for long distances, you may like to provide a more practical platform which will afford your canine passengers a comfortable, roomy bed while protecting the interior of your car. This is best made of fairly thick plywood, shaped to fit under the back squab and extending forward almost to the back of the front seats. It will need a pair of short legs at the front, which may conveniently be hinged, and, depending on the height of the ridge which normally retains the seat squab, it may need, also, a couple of blocks underneath at the back.

A puppy is sometimes unhappy in the car for the first few trips because he associates it with the pangs of leaving his puppyhood home and all the apprehensions of his new way of life; but this is soon forgotten when his stomach has settled. This uneasiness can often be helped by giving a small drink of warm water in which has been dissolved a large teaspoonful of honey or glucose, about half an hour before starting the journey. Sometimes, the white of an egg whipped up with caster sugar will settle the stomach – this slips down the throat easily too. Give the puppy a large new bone, to occupy his mind and relax his nerves. But please do not use human travel sickness cures without consulting your veterinary surgeon, as many are quite un-suitable, and may only cause further distress. If the puppy does not improve with the homely remedies, and with a few short rides to establish confidence, a tranquillizer may be prescribed. We would like to give a warning here about tranquillizers and their use. Please give these *only* under direct veterinary supervision, asking for them to be prescribed in accordance with the dog's weight. Enquire, also, how frequently the dose may be given because these drugs can have a build-up effect and if you have to make journeys on several successive days you may run into the danger of the dose having lasting effects which could even prove to be fatal.

We find it advisable to break the journey every 50 miles or so to exercise the dogs, even if only for a few minutes, if traffic is heavy and there is a lot of stop . . . go . . . stop. It relaxes the tense muscles and can prevent vomiting. On the motorway where the going is smoother, every hundred miles is all right. Occasionally, a puppy will be reassured and travel comfortably if he is in a light travelling box, but make sure that it is well ventilated and also that the draught from an open window does not blow straight in on him, or he will get either a chill or conjunctivitis, or both! A box is also advisable when he has to travel with other dogs who would not appreciate, or be improved by, his untidy motoring manners! On the other hand, as puppies tend to copy their elders, it could be that by observing the others taking car travel in their stride he will be encouraged to do likewise. In cases of persistent malaise, one can try feeding the dog some favourite goody in the car, leaving him in it without starting the engine, or even leaving him in it to sleep, if he is not inclined to be destructive. If he can spend a few short periods in the vehicle *without* feeling ill, he will soon acquire confidence for longer trips, for it is a fact that most dogs love motoring.

If this sounds like a great deal of unnecessary fuss, only remember that travel sickness is a remarkable complaint that causes an animal to suffer considerably. Also, a show dog can lose condition through vomiting and will arrive at the show thin and 'tucked up', when he can hardly be expected to give of his best in the show ring. A puppy will sometimes drool without vomiting. This produces an ugly, dark and sticky stain on his front and legs which is difficult to remove in the short time before the puppy classes begin. A large Turkish towel can be tied bib-wise about his front, and this should give him a clean start in the ring.

When a dog has to travel by air he is very seldom upset, and curiously enough, he is equally happy in the train. It is unwise to feed the dog near the starting time of his journey – a couple of hours before is best. Naturally, if a dog is travelling far he will require some food. A plastic container with a mixture of milk, water and glucose or honey, and some wheatmeal or semi-sweet biscuits are favourite snacks, also a tin (don't forget to tie on an opener) of best-quality meat if the dog will be more than twelve hours en route to his destination. For this latter we rather prefer human-consumption stewed steak, as most dog packs contain offal and this can be overpowering when opened in a warm enclosed space, as well as unappetizing to the dog.

Whenever and however the dog travels, do take care of that deadly enemy the direct draught from an open window or ventilator. If the dog is boxed, he cannot move away from it and risks a chill; if he is free, he may be foolish enough to ride with his head out of the window, and as dogs do not have eyelids to shield their eyes he can arrive with a painful case of conjunctivitis. There are several excellent ventilators on the market, all specially designed for dogs' comfort and protection. They can be inspected on the stalls at all our major shows.

16 All About Feeding

The German Shepherd Dog is not frail or difficult to keep in condition, as he is a completely natural dog in construction and coat. From a lifetime's experience, one could say that, if anything, he suffers from over-conditioning more than from actual sickness. He does not tolerate rich or heating foods, nor over-refined and unsuitable human items of 'diet' – I will not write 'nourishment' as I have the greatest contempt for the pre-packed 'easy-to-serve' stuff so widely and convincingly advertized for human consumption and deplore its use in animal feeding. It is nonsense to say that the dog prefers these 'dainties', as if he is not introduced to them (and after all, *he* doesn't watch television!) he will never be able to make comparisons with his plain, wholesome and suitable everyday food.

An adult dog has only one actual meal each day, so we must bear in mind that he really looks forward to this big moment and will show many signs of joyous anticipation for some time before the meal is given. It is almost as if he had an alarm clock which reminds him that it is dinner-time, so that if he is kept waiting he will grow restless and fretful. Therefore it is best to keep to his regular time schedule, as anxiety will not help his digestion. Dogs are very individual when it comes to feeding. A sensitive dog will eat better if he is fed alone, where there are no distracting influences or an older 'Boss Dog' of whom he is afraid. On the other hand a reluctant or unenthusiastic feeder may be stimulated by seeing another dog enjoying his dinner and perhaps making a move to help him with his when he has finished his own.

If possible, always feed him not only at the same time but also in the same place. Choose a dining place which is clean and quiet, and if it is outside, make sure that he is not uncomfortable in a cold wind or in the rain or under a hot sun. See that he has had an opportunity to attend to the wants of nature before feeding, but if he is a house pet do not shut him outside for too long or he will feel lonely and upset and disinclined to eat when he is finally let indoors with his canine sense of justice outraged.

Food bowls should be scrupulously clean, and properly scoured after each meal. For this reason, metal bowls are to be preferred to plastic material, which cannot be cleaned so thoroughly nor stand up to very hot water. It is a dreadful habit to put down food into a soiled dish left on the floor from the last meal, while to add fresh food to the remains of a previous meal is even worse; it will surely quell the appetite and eventually upset the digestion.

Care should be taken to give the food at an acceptable temperature, which is something a little more than lukewarm. Food kept under refrigeration and fed directly is one cause of gastric and other digestive disorders; it should have an hour or two to resume room temperature. Very hot food can burn a dog's sensitive mouth and scare him away from the feeding bowl. Remember that humans can take their food at a much higher temperature than dogs. We find that for puppy milk foods 65-70°F is about the correct figure.

Do not, if you can possibly avoid it, feed your dog by hand, or he will become terribly 'precious', and soon realize that he can get more attention by refusing to eat unless you are there to look after him. Naturally, if at any time your dog is unwell, you may have to tempt him, but get him back to normal as soon as possible. We have steeled ourselves not to panic if a dog should occasionally refuse one single meal, provided he has no signs of sickness, such as listlessness or coughing. If in doubt, take his temperature, which is the most reliable guide to health. Dogs are like ourselves, and have occasional days when they do not feel like eating, and then a day's rest for the digestion and stomach can do only good.

We have dealt with puppy diets, and the requirements of the growing dog in his first year, in previous chapters. The question of how much food to give the grown adult depends to a certain extent on the kind of life he leads. For example, a dog which is out all day working on a farm or walking many miles on security work can eat far more than the average house pet and still not put on too much weight. Indeed, he *needs* more food to keep him in good form for his exacting job.

Actually, we could divide the requisite amounts of food into three categories after the first twelve months. First, those of the active youngster who has ample exercise or who works at one of the several jobs in which our breed excels. One large meal when work is over, preferably fed between 4 and 6 pm, so that the dog has digested sufficiently to be alert during the night and also because this follows nature's own pattern for living, which is to go out early, run, hunt and kill, then eat and sleep. Remember, too, that regular feeding at suitable hours makes for regular elimination, which is a great convenience to owners and a big factor in keeping your dog healthy. For a dog in this bracket, we would suggest 2-2½ lb of fresh meat (i.e. horsemeat, ox heart, ox cheek and not more than half the total amount raw tripe) plus 1-2 handsful of wholewheat meal or homemade wholemeal bread rusk. If you use a proprietary brand of meal, choose one which contains yeast, as this remains crumbly and appetising when broth is poured over and does not become flat and glutinous as with non-yeast brands. To this we add one teaspoonful of olive oil, one heaped teaspoonful of seaweed powder, or the equivalent in pill form, and a dessertspoonful of finely grated carrot. Just moisten with two or three tablespoonsful of hot broth and mix up well (see page 138).

We are not advocates of the many and widely advertised additives to canine diet for the ordinary, healthy dog, although we confess to leaning heavily on the natural aids which make good the deficiencies caused by modern methods of food production. Good quality, fresh food of the kind suited to the breed should be sufficient in itself. To add all kinds of supplements causes an imbalance and does no good at all except to the manufacturers of these products. We often notice that owners seem more willing to spend money on pills than on food! Such is the pressure of present-day advertising, with its appeal to one-upmanship and easy living, often to the cost of good health.

After the first year milk is not really suitable for dogs, and we use it only as a vehicle for other foods. Milk and water in equal proportions, with a big teaspoonful of natural honey (only about ½ pint of liquid in all) is enjoyed by the dogs after their last late-night exercise, together with a small cube of cheese or of cooked liver as a 'good-night goody'.

In winter, breasts of lamb can be well boiled and fed once or twice per week. Ask your butcher not to chine them so that the large bones can be easily removed. In warm weather, you can substitute 2 lb of lightly cooked and carefully boned coley or other cheap white fish, or you can give herrings. The large bones must be removed from these last, but the small ones are not harmful. An egg yolk helps to balance this meal, mixed up with a little milk and fish liquor. Feed fish meals warm, as cold, gooey fish is unappetizing.

Bitches on active duty need the same kind of food as dogs, but give ½ lb less meat and only two *small* handsful of rusk or meal. When the bitch is on heat she may be having less exercise, in which case give only a token handful of rusk and cut down her meat by a little, say by ¼ lb. Fat built up at this time is hard to disperse, and if she is required for breeding it can be dangerous or at least make parturition difficult if she is over-weight.

Now we come to the largest category, that of the household pet and companion who lives a happy life guarding his owner's home and family and strolling around the garden. His exercise may be a short, brisk run daily with longer walks at weekends and holidays. But he sits or lies down a good deal, and unless yours is an unusual household he will get a few goodies from time to time and his 'shadow will never grow less'! For this fortunate animal, the ration is 1½ lb of fresh meat and one handful of rusk or bread, and *no* milk or honey unless he sleeps outside or in unheated quarters in winter. A weekly fast is an excellent way to keep him in trim (see chapter on weight and dieting) and he may benefit from a weekly dose of liquid paraffin (one dessertspoonful in the early morning) or the same quantity of Milk of Magnesia. A bitch living indoors will be adequately fed on 1 lb of fresh meat and a small handful of rusk.

We recommend the training classes to all owners of lone dogs. They keep the animal lively and interested and form an important part of the continuation of their socialization. The dog's appetite is frequently as much a reflection of his mental state as it is of the physical. Hunger is stimulated by a change of environment and by the effort required to work through the training programme.

An occasional change of diet is good, provided that you do not change the kind of food – *fresh* meat can be horseflesh, ox heart, ox cheek, cow beef from the knacker's yard if the source is reliable. Breast of lamb and skirt of beef are very fat, and not for regular use. Mutton, pork and poultry are totally unsuited to doggy digestions. Rabbit is for sick dogs and has a low food value and the same can be said of chicken.

Our last category is that small select band of much-loved 'oldies', many of whom are enjoying a well-deserved ease after rearing good litters or gaining a good stud record, while others have given faithful and valued companionship to their owners and are now a little tired and not quite so keen in their reactions. Old dogs can become terribly greedy. As their interest in their former active life wanes, so their attention seems to be centred on the food bowl. If the dog still takes his normal exercise and you are watchful at mealtimes (the family ones, I mean!) there is no real reason to cut down on the food intake to any extent. However, start by reducing the biscuit or rusk. This must be kept to the minimum now, although some is necessary for the proper functioning of the intestine. Fish should be given twice weekly, and topped with an egg yolk. Stop the grated carrot and double the amount of olive oil, provided there is no diarrhoea. If there is a lot of flatulence, divide the main meal into a small one at mid-day and another similar one in the early evening. The fish can be boned and cooked in the oven in milk with an egg yolk added, so that it is a sort of baked custard which is easy on the aged digestion. Most dogs love cheese, and your 'oldie' may enjoy a 4 oz carton of cottage cheese as substitute for part of the meat ration. We have great faith in yoghourt for keeping the digestion functioning and the breath sweet. A carton of natural yoghourt, 2 tablespoonsful of milk and a large teaspoonful of honey mixed in the electric blender makes an ideal supper or breakfast, or a meal for a dog with mild gastric trouble. (You can whisk it with an egg-beater if no blender is available.) Yoghourt in the small cartons is expensive, so we prepare our own with very little trouble; it is far better when made with fresh Jersey milk, and costs about half as much as the commercial variety. You need a 3-pint (at least) wide-topped Thermos vacuum jar and one carton of natural yoghourt – the best are the goatsmilk ones or 'Danone'. Bring two pints of milk to the boil, cover and let cool till you can bear your little finger in it comfortably, put the yoghourt in the rinsed-out Thermos and pour the milk over it, stirring with a wooden spoon until smooth. Cover the stopper with a piece of foil and close for six to eight hours or overnight, then remove the cork and refrigerate until thick and cold. The yoghourt mixture should never touch metal during the making.

A couple of digestive wheatmeal biscuits make a good snack for an 'oldie' on a light diet, and can be given at bedtime instead of the customary cube of liver, should this not be tolerated by the veteran. Plenty of easily digested protein and the minimum of starch will keep your old friend in good shape and pleasant to have near you to the end.

We give a few reminders of the Do's and Don'ts for all categories:

DO keep all bowls and drinking vessels clean by a daily scouring.

DO boil up the broth for moistening main meals every day, and keep the surplus under refrigeration.

DO have a large safe or cupboard with a fine-mesh, ventilated front so that all food can come up to room temperature safely away from contamination by flies.

DO feed at regular times, and weigh fish and meat for correct quantities.

DON'T feed just before or immediately after violent exercise. Allow half an hour's breathing space either side of the meal, even in the case of walking.

DON'T feed after your own mealtime if the dog is a house pet and can see your own food prepared and served. Feed him first – and it is better to keep him out of the family dining-room.

DON'T keep uneaten food. If the meal is uneaten after a reasonable time, take it up and throw it away, and feed the next meal a little earlier than usual.

DON'T deprive your dog of water unless he is sick and the veterinary surgeon advises it. We often hear that water should be withheld before or after food, but our own considered opinion is that, provided that fresh water in clean containers is always available, dogs are sensible enough not to drink when it is harmful. Water is essential to a dog, and to keep him thirsty is extremely cruel. He can go without food for quite long periods without undue suffering, but even a short period without water is damaging to his health.

DON'T withhold food as a punishment. If your dog has offended, make your peace with him before his dinner-time and feed him normally. He will only be made miserable by what is really unfair treatment, since he can never understand the connection between his sins and his hunger. He can connect a goody with work or with training progress, and will understand that he has to behave to obtain his reward. He expects to be fed by you when he is hungry, however, and with no strings attached. His behaviour must be corrected independently of his stomach.

17 All About General Health and Sickness

Properly fed and exercised, ours is a tough and healthy breed with a good record among the veterinary profession for its courage in illness and excellent powers of recovery.

Although a German Shepherd can and does endure severe weather conditions and still remain healthy, he will keep fit only when he has sufficient freedom and exercise to stimulate his circulation and maintain his muscles in firm, supple order. If he lies about outside, particularly on cold concrete, or is left for long periods in a cold, draughty kennel, he will soon fall a victim to a disease he is prone to develop, i.e. rheumatism in all its painful forms. The symptoms are similar to those in humans, swelling and stiffness of the joints affected, and the victim may cry with pain when getting up or down. If simple treatment is given early, the attack may wear off or at least be alleviated, so that the dog only suffers an occasional twinge. One aspirin or Veganin tablet only may be given night and morning. Dogs do not tolerate aspirin in the same quantities as humans can so do not exceed this dose except under veterinary advice. A dose of one dessertspoonful of Milk of Magnesia to keep any toxic condition under control is helpful, and can be given three times weekly with a day's interval between each dose. A course of Denes' greenleaf tablets is also beneficial in acid conditions caused by rheumatism (or vice versa). The sleeping quarters must be checked for any draughts or dampness; raise the bed from floor level and give some light, cosy bedding – wood-wool is especially suitable. If you suspect a draught overhead, rig a canopy over the sleeping bench with a blanket slung over lengths of expanding curtain-runners or strong cord. If these homely remedies do not bring relief in a reasonable time, you must seek professional advice, as the dreaded hip dysplasia and rheumatism have several symptoms in common, and only an X-ray picture can supply the answer.

Skin ailments come a close second in frequency. Sudden bursts of enthusiastic scratching usually indicate the presence of fleas, but slow, constant rhythmic scratching is a sign that all is not well with the dog's skin and a careful examination is necessary. Put the dog on a table or bench, if possible, or stretch him out on the floor, and then go over him carefully with a steel comb, parting the hair everywhere and inspecting under the elbows and the flanks for sore places or a rash. If taken early, the majority of skin troubles respond quickly to simple treatment. Cut out all starch from the diet for a week or ten days, and dab any red places or spots with calamine lotion several times a day, taking care that the dog does not lick the lotion, which always makes him sick. The diet must be checked, as perhaps the quality or type of meat has varied, and the dog does not tolerate his present kind of meat. A day's fast is usually helpful (see chapter 10) and no rusk or other starch, and also no milk, should be given until he is well again. Naturally, if there is no sign of improvement after a few days, you must call in your veterinary surgeon.

At any time when your dog appears unwell it is wise to take his temperature. Keep a rectal thermometer for this purpose, and learn to read it correctly so that you can record it for the veterinary surgeon's information at any time. The normal reading for an adult dog is 101.2°F, although a young puppy can register 102.2°F without being ill. Unless the dog is very quiet, it is better to have help to control him, as a broken thermometer can be quite dangerous. If you can persuade the dog to lie on his side it will be easier, then, having greased the bulb with white vaseline and noted that it has been properly shaken down from previous use, insert it gently into the rectum and hold it firmly until the full record time is up. As a dog cannot tell you, except in a general manner, that he is not feeling well, the thermometer is your best help in obtaining an early diagnosis to be followed, we hope, by a swift recovery.

The root cause of much canine sickness is constipation. Modern feeding methods do little to improve matters here. All food which is preserved or processed lacks the natural bulk which is so essential to the proper functioning of the dog's intestine. If you add to this handicap the sometimes (alas, too often!) 'kind' owner who feeds refined human foods containing white flour and sugar, dried milk, etc. and which are made tasty with seasoning and additives, all calculated to ruin a dog's appetite for his own suitable diet, then it is small wonder that the dog's intestine is blocked and the dog ailing.

An experienced breeder always notes the state of the dog's daily eliminations. The stool should be passed easily and without undue straining and be a normal brown colour. Light or 'clay' colour indicates a liver disturbance, and possibly a chill. Black or very dark colour is a sign of bowel haemorrhage, and your veterinary surgeon should check this soon.

For the liver condition, unless the dog appears to be suffering badly, you can overcome the attack by stopping all fats, oils and milk and giving him two or three tablespoonsful of finely grated carrot, well incorporated in fresh minced meat. If he is hungry he will not notice the carrot and you may have to keep him on this for a few days until normality is restored. A course of Denes' parsley and watercress pills is beneficial for liver trouble. If the dog is eager for more food, give him a natural yoghourt blended with a teaspoonful of honey for breakfast, and unless there are other symptoms step up his daily exercise which will do much to help him shake off his trouble.

Should you notice that his stools are dry and crumbly or hard packed, he requires a dessertspoonful of liquid paraffin early each morning for two or three days, and a similar quantity of olive oil in his dinner. If there is straining without faeces being passed, it is most likely that the dog has a slight stoppage caused either by fragments of chewed-up bone, or from eating rubbish which he may have found or stolen. This can be cleared by giving an enema, preferably from a gravity-flow douche can. A pint of lukewarm water with a tablespoonful of olive oil in it is about the correct amount. Lubricate the nozzle, and let the liquid flow very slowly, with frequent pauses, into the rectum. If you can stand the dog with his hind legs higher than his front ones it will help the water to penetrate. Have plenty of newspaper ready, as the results come immediately. Rest the dog afterwards and feed lightly, adding a tablespoonful of All-Bran or similar health cereal to his food until the eliminations are performed easily and normally again.

Most digestive and gastric complaints can be quickly ended if treatment is given immediately symptoms are noticed. A day's fast on water with honey or glucose, thus completely resting the whole system, brings surprisingly good results in the majority of cases. There is no real cause for alarm if the dog does not eat any solid food for thirty-six to forty-eight hours, provided he is kept well supplied with fluids. The milk, water and honey drink, beef tea, strained chicken and rice broth are all suitable. Diarrhoea is another sign that all is not well internally. The causes are many and varied, and although in small puppies it is often just teething troubles and rarely lasts more than a day or so, the older dog must be kept under close observation and his temperature taken and recorded. Should the reading remain high for twenty-four hours, or other symptoms develop, it is time to call your veterinary surgeon. For straightforward diarrhoea, this simple remedy is effective more often than not. Take two tablespoonfuls of cornflour or arrowroot and moisten with cold water to a thin paste in a thick bowl, preferably of metal. Pour on boiling water, stirring quickly, until it clears like old-fashioned laundry starch. Add two or three tablespoonsful of white sugar and three or four tablespoonsful of evaporated milk and cool it well – an eggwhisk will keep it from thickening too much. This drink can be repeated two or three times during the day until the condition clears up, or with puppies it can be substituted for their normal milk feeds.

Pancreatic Insufficiency (or malabsorbtion) is a disease common to most breeds; but seems to be most prevalent in the German Shepherd Dog. It is an abnormality of the small intestine, or pancreas, which prevents the proper absorbtion of food. The symptoms are usually diaorrhea, or frequent passing of faeces, with accompanying great loss of weight and condition. A great deal of useful research is still going on, with excellent results: and highly specialised studies are being made by top veterinary professors. Usually, a fat-free diet, with no milk, is prescribed; but veterinary advice and proper tests are recommended immediately such symptoms are noticed.

Sore throats and coughs are also sometimes indications of more serious illness such as bronchitis, so they should never be neglected. If the dog coughs and seems worried and paws at his mouth or neck, it may be that he has something lodged in his throat. Open his mouth wide and shine a bright flashlight down his throat, exploring gently with your finger for a piece of bone or wood or any other object which he may have scavenged and swallowed. If anything is found in the throat, get the sufferer quickly to his veterinary surgeon, as the tender membranes of the mouth and throat could be damaged if interfered with by anyone other than a qualified practitioner. A fish-bone, however, can often be pushed down the gullet and out of harm's way by forcing a piece of soft, crustless bread down the throat – a piece half the size of a hen's egg will be right. Meanwhile, massage the throat and neck very gently and carefully, to persuade the dog to swallow.

A dry, hacking cough which persists, particularly at night, although there is no temperature nor loss of appetite, is most likely to be what is known as Kennel Cough or, more properly, Tracheobronchitis, which is fairly common in young puppies. This cough is not really dangerous, but it is highly infectious and very tiring to young dogs. We like our veterinary surgeon to give two doses of antibiotic by injection, with an interval in between, while we help by giving small and frequent doses of honey, lemon juice and glycerine in equal quantities and well shaken up. A teaspoonful put well back in the throat will soothe the soreness, and as it contains no drugs it can be used freely.

If your dog coughs after contracting a chill, smear a little camphorated oil on his chest, so that he inhales the vapour, which should soothe him.

Another cause of soreness, which gives the apparent symptoms of a heavy catarrhal cold, is stinging from nettles. In themselves, with their thick coats, the dogs do not feel the stings, but if they run to hunt among the nettles, the nose and lips can be stung and become very swollen, which may affect the throat. Nupercainal ointment (CIBA) contains a small amount of cocaine which deadens the pain and allows healing to start if a little is smeared on the affected parts.

A warm bed and rest are always recommended for a sick dog. Unless the weather is very cold do not use artificial heat, but give a snug bed well away from draughts and raised up from the floor. One has only to see the delight dogs have in tunnelling a large hole to lie in to appreciate their preference for a 'den'. As really sick animals are usually nursed indoors for convenience, a heavy chair placed either side of the patient's bed, with two strong cords stretched across and a blanket slung over them, will make an ideal den and encourage the sufferer to rest quietly. We find this better than placing the bed near any kind of heating apparatus or fire, as he will soon move away from direct heat to seek a cool spot, which is in direct opposition to his requirements.

Fits and convulsions are the most alarming of all illnesses, and we recommend all owners to familiarize themselves with the immediate treatment so as to avoid distress and possible danger from a dog who is temporarily not himself. Occasionally puppies have convulsions during their teething periods, or again when they are at the stage of rapid growth which has gone beyond their strength and put a strain on their systems. During the convulsion the puppy may snap or behave in an unpredictable manner, so quickly cover his head with a towel or light blanket (or a jacket in an emergency) and transfer him at once to a darkened room or a small kennel where there is nothing he might knock down to injure himself. Keeping him out of a direct bright light is an essential part of the 'first-aid'. The presence of worms or a dietary deficiency can sometimes cause fits, and long and unaccustomed sojourns under a hot sun will also affect a puppy (sunstroke).

As a general guide to the possible causes of fits, we consider that should the puppy lose consciousness during the attack he probably has some brain damage caused by the virus-borne disease encephalitis, but if he retains awareness of people around him it may be due to any of the aforementioned causes, or to some toxin from rubbish devoured during scavenging.

One can expect an easy recovery from the attacks caused by worms or food toxins, once they have been diagnosed and corrected. However, any convulsions stemming from a virus are very troublesome and invariably cause nerve damage and chorea (sometimes known as 'twitches'). If the treatment is immediate and there is no history of similar illness in the puppy's forbears, the nervous symptoms may disappear with maturity, but there is, unfortunately, no certain cure, nor can one tell to what extent the nervous system has suffered from the attacks. During the recovery period, a bland diet of easily assimilated food is recommended to rest the digestion. The porridge made from semolina (see the chapter on puppy rearing), honey and milk, egg yolk and milk custard, cottage cheese, yoghourt and fish are all excellent light nourishment. A few wheatmeal digestive biscuits will round out the diet if the patient seems hungry. Your veterinary surgeon will most likely prescribe bromide, or some similar sedative, and dosage will follow the nature and severity of the illness. The sufferer will have to be kept very quiet and away from teasing companions meanwhile.

Teething convulsions in an otherwise healthy puppy are most likely to be slight affairs and can be dealt with by a soothing dose of a large teaspoonful of Milk of Magnesia early each morning for three days, to be followed after a two-day interval by another three doses. It helps the puppy at this time to have a large, hard bone to chew on to keep his mind off the pain and relax his nerves.

One other dangerous convulsion which can occur in a newly whelped bitch is known as eclampsia. This distressing attack is caused by a shortage of calcium, which has been drained from the system during the period of gestation and the early feeding of a lusty litter. If this happens, remove the puppies quickly and telephone your veterinary surgeon for help. Keep her very quiet until help arrives, and try to get three or four calcium or bone meal tablets crushed up in milk down her throat. The vet will probably give an intravenous injection of calcium, which should quickly put matters right again. Meanwhile, you must feed the puppies on evaporated milk diluted in warm water and with glucose added; suggested proportions are two tablespoonfuls of evaporated milk, ½ pint of water and a heaped teaspoonful of glucose. The puppies will be quite safe for eight to twelve hours provided they are kept warm and not allowed to dehydrate, and by then the mother will most likely have recovered when they can be restored to her care, or you will have had time to seek a foster-mother. The mother will naturally require your attentive care for a few days, and you could ask the veterinary surgeon to check for acid milk condition.

We can scarcely call vomiting an illness, but it is a sign of internal upset in many cases. Country dogs are often sick after eating grass or green oats, which they eat with such pleasure. It is curious how animals know what is beneficial to them when they are given the opportunity to seek it. Some years ago all our bitches had regular feasts on the leaves of a plant called Wood Betony, and enquiries revealed that herbalists prescribe it for female troubles, and that gypsies make tea from it for the same purpose! Food fed too cold from refrigeration can also be thrown back by a dog, and even copious draughts of very cold water after violent exercise can be rejected. But the vomiting of mucousy liquid, together with an excessive thirst, indicates a gastric condition, and you will be wise to seek professional advice at once, keeping the sufferer warm and giving only sips of milk and honey – no water should be available to the dog until diagnosis has been made.

With the efficacy of modern inoculations and the almost total use of immunisation, we find that few people have ever had to deal with a case of either of the dreaded killer diseases of distemper and hepatitis.

Distemper attacks the central nervous system and hepatitis the liver; there is really no known cure for either, and both are virus diseases. A discharge from the eyes and nose like a heavy cold, diarrhoea and vomiting, accompanied by a rocketing temperature, are the obvious signs of both diseases. The subsequent course and development of the illness varies sufficiently for each case to be treated individually, and a helpful veterinary surgeon can sometimes bring an animal through, albeit only rarely unscathed. A cruel feature of distemper is that the poor dog may make a brief recovery for a few days, only to succumb to pneumonia or chorea. An adult dog which survives two or three days of hepatitis may make a fair recovery. One alarming feature is that one or both eyes may turn an opaque blue colour following the attack. This is not permanent, however, and usually clears up within a week.

These are most highly contagious diseases, and if you are unfortunate enough to have to nurse a case, the strictest precautions have to be taken should you also have other dogs. All clothing, particularly shoes and stockings, must be changed before going near any other dogs, and they must be kept as far as possible from the infected one.

Another very dangerous disease is leptospirosis, which is an infectious jaundice sometimes known in England as Miners' Disease. It is carried by rats (also by foxes) and these could run over the snack meals which miners used to take down below with them and so pass on the infection. The virus is, in fact, carried by the urine. The attack is extremely painful and hard in recovery, the loss of weight being very difficult to make up again. There are actually two types of leptospirosis, canicola and icterhaemorrhagiae, and initially they appear to have the same symptoms as distemper. The incubation period is approximately one to two weeks, allowing a day on either side. Loss of appetite with the resultant weakness, vomiting, and a rectal thermometer reading of 103°F – 105°F are the usual signs, but when he first falls ill the dog will suffer a considerable drop in temperature and will seem listless and downcast with laborious breathing. He will also have a terrific thirst, something we do not often see with distemper sufferers. There is a stiffness and pain in all limbs, particularly if the dog has been sitting; he may even be temporarily unable to move. Parvo-virus is a present day killer disease in puppies, symptoms being vomiting, diarrhoea and often complete collapse, an urgent call to your veterinary surgeon is your best hope for recovery.

All the foregoing is really a warning to breeders and owners. First of all, to see that cleanliness and thorough disinfection are priorities in the kennel. Then, always to be on good terms with your veterinary surgeon so that he fully understands your case and is willing to make arrangements to come to your aid immediately in an emergency such as any of the above. These people lead busy lives with irregular hours, so that a cup of tea or coffee ready to hand as they discuss the case is usually acceptable.

When it comes to convalescence after any serious illness, the owner is really put to the test in patience and skill, as the period of recovery can be long and tedious. The strong tie of affection between owner and dog does much to get the dog back on his feet, and one is so amply rewarded in seeing the dog once again enjoying the vigorous health which is really part of the Shepherd Dog. Food in convalescence can be a problem. It must be light, nourishing and easily digested but also, unfortunately, of a bland nature so that the patient is quickly disinterested. We suggest the following items of convalescent diet. Scramble some egg yolks with a little butter and some cows' milk (goats' milk is better if you can get it) and add a few crisp dried wholemeal breadcrumbs to the mixture, with a little honey or, alternatively, a tablespoonful of finely grated cheese. Boil an old hen for several hours with onions, carrots and garlic (but no green vegetables, which give terrible flatulence). Bone off the meat and either chop it or mince it and mix with a few dried breadcrumbs. This is usually tasty enough to tempt the convalescent animal. Boil the remainder of the stock and strain it over two envelopesful of powdered gelatine, which is a delicate and easily assimilated form of protein. It will gel in the refrigerator, and a little given to a feverish dog is usually eagerly licked and helps to bring down the temperature. You can make beef jelly in a similar manner, shredding up 1 lb of lean shin of beef, removing both skin and any fat. Cover with a good pint of water and put in a stone jar or strong basin which you stand in a pan of hot water and cook covered in the bottom oven of an Aga or in a low-heated gas or electric oven for several hours, pressing the meat with a fork against the basin side occasionally to extract the juice. Finally, strain through a coarse strainer. It can be offered lukewarm to the sick dog or poured over one envelopeful (½ oz size) of gelatine and given cold. Do *not* use the ready prepared chicken or beef cubes, as they are very salt and contain flavouring and preservatives which might irritate a tender digestion.

We have found plain ice-cream excellent for a dog with a high temperature – the best quality vanilla or, best of all, homemade with fresh eggs and cream and flavoured with honey. Even a dangerously sick dog rarely refuses to lick this, and it can make the difference of life or death when the dog's temperature soars and dehydration has occurred.

We cannot end this chapter without a reference, albeit reluctant, to hip dysplasia. So much has been written by experts and despite this there are still so many schools of thought that we prefer to keep an open mind on the subject or, at least, not to be too definite in our opinions. As our breed is the largest numerically, it follows that it has the largest number of hip-dysplastic dogs. Then, since the breed is often called to work, it is more often examined for the trouble than other breeds, more records are kept of the number of suspects and so the legend grows that the breed is riddled with the defect, which is far from the actual truth.

The investigation into hip dysplasia began in the USA in the early 1950s. I was judging our breed at the great Morris and Essex Show in 1952, and caught the first full salvo in the continuing controversy. It struck me then, as it does now, that too many voices were raised, and many of them not in a disinterested manner, for any good to come out of the several systems devised to check, control and even 'cure' the disease. Veterinary research has made some progress, and investigation has revealed that many other breeds have a higher percentage of the incidence of dysplasia than our own. These breeds have also, in many cases, instituted research into the disease.

In our own breed we are fortunate in having a parent club (the S.V.) which guards the German Shepherd Dog's interests more strictly perhaps than any other breed club (witness the great demands made on the breeders in their breed survey and the rules controlling breeding). However, despite their vigilance, the S.V. are mindful of the fact that breeding Shepherd Dogs is, for most of us, a hobby, and only when it is essential do they enforce a rule which has been made to safeguard the breed so that we may continue to enjoy our dogs and their enviable reputation as the world's No. 1 choice for service dogs. In Germany, 95 per cent of the police dogs are German Shepherds, and it is hardly likely that such an almost unanimous choice would be made from a breed that was unsound or unfit, since their life is a hard and demanding one, both physically and mentally. In 1966 the S.V. decided, after years of patient research and proper deliberation, to allow dogs which had been satisfactorily X-rayed under their supervision (there are breed surveyors in each district in Germany) to be tattooed on the ear with an identification number to correspond with their registration number and the number on the X-ray plates, and to issue gradings starting with 'a' for all clear. This would seem to us to do away with many of the loopholes and much of the suspicion surrounding the issue. Our own Kennel Club also has a scheme for the X-ray examination and issues in the *Kennel Club Gazette* a list of those dogs which have been cleared. A Breeder's Letter is also issued in respect of those dogs which are not absolutely clear but are passed as sound enough for breeding. We would guess that there are many thousands in this latter bracket.

The German Shepherd League of Great Britain has inherited a scheme from the former Breed Improvement movement whereby breeders can have X-rays examined and graded to mark the degree of hip dysplasia recorded on the plate. A number of owners/breeders have availed themselves of this facility, but it is entirely voluntary and is done for the owner's satisfaction. All steps taken to produce soundness and health in our dogs are to be applauded and hip dysplasia is one of the many points in our rapidly increasing breed where education and enlightenment are required. The scheme, in the writer's opinion, ranks in importance alongside correct feeding and exercising as well as understanding, maintenance and training.

For ourselves, we are bound to say we treat hip dysplasia like any other unsoundness. If it is clinically noticeable we don't breed with such animals. We feed and exercise our dogs in such a way as to satisfy to the maximum the requirements for good muscles and firmness of limbs and character. Although in our innermost selves we do not accept that hip dysplasia is hereditary, we would always prefer to use a dog which had the coveted pass, to see if we can improve (and we usually can), and we would never knowingly be involved in breeding from an unsound bitch.

18 All About the Old German Shepherd Dog

This is a tearful chapter for us all, as there are few owners, if any, who do not dread the passing years which all too quickly turn our naughty, endearing puppy into a sedate matron or a dignified daddy. We could not consider ours as a long-lived breed (with a few notable exceptions) and the go-slow period begins at about their eighth year, when it is time to watch their diet, exercise and above all the warmth and comfort of their sleeping quarters, so that rheumatism does not add to the other discomforts of increasing years.

See Chapter 16 about feeding the cherished 'oldie'. Make a regular check-up on teeth and ears, and have any loose or badly decayed teeth removed by the veterinary surgeon. The ears should be carefully cleaned of all hard wax, which can be painful and make the dog miserable and inclined to snap if he is jostled by other dogs. In fact, it is better if he can be given a quiet place of his own where he can, if he wishes, keep away from the lively, teasing youngsters, and where he can rest since old dogs sleep a good deal. However, do not banish him from the scene so that he feels lonely, or he may pine.

A very old dog may become deaf or suffer from failing eyesight. If he is not in any pain, he will not be distressed, as it has probably been a progressive deterioration and he has adjusted himself naturally. If he remains in his old familiar surroundings, he will find his way about without difficulty.

Use a fairly soft brush for grooming now, and if the coat requires cleansing use one of the several commercial dry shampoos, as bathing can be dangerous to our oldies. If the breath is unpleasant, give a chlorophyll tablet once or twice per day, and see that his eliminations are regular and normal. Small doses (or tablets) of Milk of Magnesia can be helpful, and from time to time a dessertspoonful of liquid paraffin.

La Martine, the famous French writer and poet, wrote: 'Quand l'homme est triste, le bon Dieu l'envoit un chien' (When Man is sad, the good Lord sends him a dog). He did not, however, say how much sadder Man can be when he loses his dog, nor offer any remedy, as indeed nobody can, since losing one's dog is a terrible personal grief which is always difficult to accept. However, if the much-loved old friend weakens in constitution, or loses the use of his hind-quarters, or if he can no longer be trusted about the house, then make up your mind to help him on his way before real suffering and distress make his

The Old Dog
'With eye upraised his master's look to scan,
The joy, the solace and the aid of man,
The rich man's guardian and the poor man's friend,
The only being faithful to the end.'

                    Crabbe

end dreadful for you both. Your trusted veterinary surgeon will give him a peaceful and completely pain-free passing while you feed him some favourite tit-bit. Many people prefer to give a couple of sleeping tablets before the veterinary surgeon arrives, so that the end is merely a continuation of sleep.

It is really self-indulgence to keep a feeble or badly ailing animal alive just because one has not the courage to take the decision. It is the last kindness one can do for him, and even when grief is sharpest one feels better for knowing he no longer suffers. Afterwards, it is better to go away for a day or so, or call on sympathetic friends. If he was your only canine companion, pay him the compliment of replacing him promptly – it is the best 'thank you' for his love and devotion and a tribute to the breed he has caused you to adopt as your own. This is one argument for buying a first puppy from an established kennel with its own blood-line, since there is usually a puppy of similar breeding and appearance to fill the gap left by your old friend.

19 Something About Present-day Top Dogs

A chapter is not long enough to give more than an indication of the influence of some present-day winners upon the breed. The illustrations speak for themselves so far as type is concerned, and the dogs' records in the show ring and their breeding results will support their claims to being notable German Shepherd Dogs. Foremost of the active competitors in the ring at the time of writing (1979) was surely Champion Delridge Erhard, with 23 C.C.s and 10 res. C.C.s. He is the sire, to date, of two dog Champions, Ramadan Jacobus and Royvons Red Rum, and two bitch Champions, Fairy Cross Made to Measure and Sadira Paulette, in Great Britain; of one dog Champion, Vaalhoek Erick of Lascala C.D.Ex, and one bitch Champion, Gorsefield Chantal, in South Africa; and of one bitch Champion in Australia,

Champion Delridge Erhard by Vegrin Erhard ex Delridge Camilla. Born 12 October 1973. With 23 C.C.s and 10 Reserves in 1979 Erhard was a strong link in the breed's progress towards a more compact animal, and shows the high withers and longer front legs inherited from his maternal grandfather, Jugolands Lothar.

Judamie Atstanya. This line is extended in Royvons Red Rum, the youngest post-war Champion in the breed, being made up at only 14 months, and with 46 C.C.s and 10 res. C.C.s in 1985. Another dominant descendant is Ch. Ramadan Jacobus, whose son Ch. Voirlich Amigus was Best in Show at the G.S.D. League's Diamond Jubilee Show in summer 1979. Erhard's dam, Delridge Camilla, is a remarkable brood bitch; in her litter to International Champion Druidswood Consort she produced Ch. Delridge Indigo.

English, Australian and New Zealand Champion Rossfort Premonition is perhaps the best known of the Champions of recent years, the sire of many Champions and top winners on both sides of the world. He was exported to New Zealand when seven years old – a great loss to the show ring here. Premonition, through his sire Lex of Glanford, is a grandson of Ilk v. Eschbacher Klippen SchH I.

Druidswood Consort was one of the few British-bred International Champions in post-war years. He sired 14 Champions in his short life, and is the grandsire of both Red Rum and Amigus, pictured here. Others were Gorsefield Granit, Consort's grandsire, a truly classic dog and one of the breed's Greats; and latterly Rothwick Invictor, bred by Mrs Ringwald. His influence on construction and character has been widespread.

Champion Royvons Red Rum by Ch. Delridge Erhard ex Caemaen Kendra of Bridgecroft. Born 3 June 1977. Owned and bred by Yvonne and Roy James.

Champion Voirlich Amigus by Ch. Ramadan Jacobus ex Castelmaine Mercedes. Born 25 January 1977. At only two years of age this handsome dog won B.I.S. at the German Shepherd Dog League's Diamond Jubilee Show in 1979. Owned and bred by Mrs Jill Warner.

English and Irish Champion Druidswood Consort by Dromcot Quadra of Charoan ex Druidswood Yasmin. Born 15 April 1968. Sire of 14 Champions by 1980, Consort is widely noted for his beautiful head and rich sable colouring. Owned by Mrs M. A. Spencer. Bred by Mrs M. Pickup.

Champion Cito von Königsbruch by Nick von der Wienerau ex Biene vom Entlebuch. Owned by Paul and Tracey Bradley.

Dick di Quattroville SchH II. By Double Sieger Uran von Wildsteigerland SchH III ex Moira di Ca San Marco SchH II. Owned by Standahl Kennels Ltd.

In Germany the reigning king of the breed is undoubtedly the 1978 Sieger, Canto Arminius, a dog of perfect proportions with a wonderful character and working ability. Canto is a grandson, through his sire Canto v. d. Wienerau, of Hein v. Konigsbruch, who was imported and left behind him some excellent stock and a reputation for temperament and character which earned him a special place in the German hierarchy here.

Some very good dogs have come here from Germany in recent years, and have influenced the breed beneficially. Amongst these I would mention Champion Joll v. Bemholt SchH III, who has proved a good producer in the training world, too, as was to be expected from his background. Ch. Cito v. Königsbruch is the most recent successful stud dog, having sired nearly 20 champions. Two of his progeny are pictured here. Imported from Germany he has shown a remarkable consistency in his offspring from bitches of a variety of bloodlines. We must not forget the beautiful Sieger Mutz a. d. Kuckstrasse, whose picture still adorns all the S.V. gatherings as the ideal dog. Mutz sired some attractive animals during his brief period at stud here.

This short list has obviously not included all the many winning dogs of recent years; any omissions are not intentional. The aim has been to create an image of the breed as it is today, with some of the animals which have contributed to what is not an unsatisfactory picture where type and soundness are concerned, and reflects well on the British breeder's discernment of a good breeding animal of whatever nationality.

Champion Moonwinds Golden Harrier born 12 December 1982.
By Ch. Cito v. Königsbruch ex Moonwinds Golden Cloudburst.
Owned and bred by Miss P. Meaton.

Champion Donzarra's Erla born 14 January 1982.
By Ch. Cito v. Königsbruch ex Treavons Wild Alliance of Donzarra.
Owned and bred by Sean and Sue Disney.

20 A Little About the German Qualifications and How These Are Obtained

There are so many training qualifications and working degrees in Germany that we feel a list of them would be interesting, particularly to the large number who visit the Hauptzuchtschau, so that one can more easily assess a dog which takes the fancy. In fact, each qualification reflects the development of the German Shepherd Dog through the basic organization of the S. V., and as they are somewhat different from our own English ones, a short description will be given. To begin with, no dog can be entered in Adult (Open) classes under S.V. rules that is not two years old or more and that has no working qualification. From this one can gather that the dog with the best breeding is the one with the greatest number of working qualifications on his pedigree, as all his forebears had to be qualified so that they could be entered for show competition. This is how the S.V. makes certain that intelligence and beauty are never separated in their stock, as it is virtually impossible to make up a top winner in beauty without his having working degrees indicating strong character, as we will explain. It is exceptional to see an animal without working qualifications on a well-known dog's pedigree, as these are valued at least as highly as beauty prizes in breed classes. However, there are a few owners living in remote parts who do not have the opportunity of showing their stock, so one can occasionally find one of these otherwise excellent dogs in a pedigree.

We give here a brief explanation of some of the degrees most frequently encountered. First we are bound to note HGH, which is the abbreviation for Herdengebrauchshund or working shepherd dog, and this can be won only at the separate trials held for actual sheep-herding animals. Very large numbers of spectators attend these important events, the standard of work is extremely high and the interest in the keen competition is very great. We always wish that more publicity was given to this aspect of our breed's work, particularly in Great Britain. It might help to improve the image of the German Shepherd Dog.

The Ausdauer Prüfung (AD) causes much interest in Great Britain as we have no test remotely resembling it. Briefly, the adult dog has to run beside a bicycle for 20 kilometres, with halts at certain stages to ascertain that his feet are not damaged or causing him pain, when he would instantly be withdrawn. At the end of the 20 kilometres, after a brief pause, he must do some simple obedience tests to show that he has not been mentally affected by the long run. He is examined by vererinary surgeons and senior S.V. officials, his heart and lungs are tested and his feet carefully scrutinized, and his temperament re-assessed, since as we have often pointed out, physical beauty and even toughness are considered by the Germans only when the dog has the correct German Shepherd character. One could say that a dog which comes through such a gruelling test is indeed worthy of his name.

Almost without exception, the well-known dogs have SchH, which stands for Schutzhund, guard dog. After SchH we see the ratings of I, II, or III. The training is arduous and the standard of work required to gain any of these degrees very high indeed. The dogs are gun-tested at the start of the 'heel free' exercise, and any which react badly are rated gun-shy (Schussgleichgültig) and are immediately eliminated; no further time is wasted on them. SchH I is for dogs from the age of fourteen months, SchH II is for dogs from the age of sixteen months, the two tests being similar with a maximum of 100 marks in each. SchH III is for dogs from twenty months and is a very hard and comprehensive test. There is a compulsory six weeks' interval between entry for each grade. If a dog fails to obtain a minimum of 80 per cent marks in the man-work section, it must be taken again if he is to qualify 'good'. The heel work in SchH III is sensational to watch as it is done free, without commands from judge or steward, and here the handler really comes into his own, putting up a great show with the dog working heel free. It is one of the requirements in the Open classes at the Siegerschau, and is always a pleasure to watch. Thus you may be certain that any dog displaying the above-mentioned letters after his name has a fearless character and is thoroughly well-trained.

A qualification essentially German and which requires a little explanation to our newcomers is the word Angekoert (sometimes written Angekört). When you see a German show catalogue, you will notice before many dog's names an 'x'. This means that they are Angekoert, the translation of which is 'breed surveyed'. In other words, they have been examined by the breed survey. You will see that many of the German qualifications have no connection with obedience or trials work except indirectly, since they indicate character and stamina – two absolute 'MUSTS' in our Shepherd Dog anywhere. At the breed survey, the animal is given a complete and exhaustive examination, even weighed and measured, and every point and detail is noted, before it is passed or rejected for breeding. When an animal is passed, the qualification gives indications as to which blood-lines are harmonious with this animal, and which are unsuitable and to be avoided. This is to prevent inbreeding on similar faults, such as two lines which give soft ears, or two others with faulty mouths. It also recommends the proper use of the dog's virtues in mating like to like – that is to say, perhaps, good shoulders to good shoulders and strong pigment to strong pigment (the late and much missed Nem Elliott was always expounding this theory).

In case you should wonder why, or whether, breeders trouble themselves with the findings of the reports issued by the Koermeister, let us hasten to say that nobody would get very far with a breeding programme should he ignore the essential directive of the Koerung. A complete impasse would be reached in the show ring, where the handler must show the dog's pedigree and all documents relating to his breeding and training. If the animal is not bred to the correct pattern he will never achieve top honours however beautiful or intelligent he may be!

If you should buy a puppy which has imported parents, or should you be considering a German import as a mate for your bitch, you may see a German pedigree when you are shown the blood-lines. These pedigrees are vastly different from our own, so we will give some explanations of this large, comprehensive document, full of the most detailed notes on the dog such as we are not fortunate enough to see on our own pedigrees, and since all information is checked at S.V. headquarters there is no possible chance of a false pedigree being issued.

The dog's name, sex, colour and marking, also any distinctive features and the full date of birth are noted. Then the breeder's name and a listed line-breeding. An interesting addition is the complete information on the litter-mates, their registered names and colours and the number of puppies in the litter. It also states whether more than the six puppies allowed by the S.V. rules were reared and, if this was so, how many by the natural mother and how many by the foster-mother (this is permitted, provided notice is given to the local breed warden). As well as the dog's registered number, the volume of the stud-book in which he is entered is given. In addition to the breeder's signature, certifying the authenticity of the information, there is the S.V.'s declaration that all details on the pedigree have been checked and found to be correct, together with the date and serial number of the registration. There is a space with the directive that the certificate must be validated by the S.V. when the dog is 18 months old. This validation is for the dog's entire life, and is stamped in red across the vacant space 'Auf Lebenzeit Verlängert', meaning extension for life. However, before this extension can be obtained the owner must produce for the S. V. a satisfactory report from an 'examiner for young dogs' qualified by the S.V. or a show report where the dog has received a rating of 'Gut' (good) or perhaps even higher for conformation. Also noted on this page of the pedigree is the dog's breed survey rating (Koervermerke). For example, this could read 'Angekoert 1969-70 I', which conveys that the dog has been examined at the survey and passed Class I, and is thus approved for breeding for those years. In the autumn of 1970 he would again have to be presented to the Koermeister, who may give an extension of the approval for a period of up to four years, which would bring the dog up to his eighth year. Should he still be in good shape at this age he may be given a one-year extension, and thereafter have to be presented each year for further examination for a possible renewal of the Koermeister's approval.

It can be plainly seen how the breed is controlled by the enforcement of such measures. The difference between Koer-klasse I and II is that in the No. I grading the dog had an 'especial recommendation for breeding', while in No. II he is graded 'suitable for breeding', which could signify that he has a couple of minor faults of construction (or a missing premolar) but has won his approval for use because of his good blood-lines or his working performance. It can happen that a dog improves enough between the examinations to qualify for a Class I grading at the next presentation.

Inside the document there is a four-generation pedigree of the dog, back to his great-great-great-grandparents, with much useful information about these forebears, including their colour and markings ('Farbe' and 'Abzeichen'), together with the breed survey reports of the two closest generations and a description of all the litter-mates of these six dogs, stating whether they, too, have been surveyed and their highest ratings at shows. All the dogs' names and training degrees are given, which makes it a true breeder's guide when planning a litter or founding a blood-line. All this information is 100 per cent reliable, having been checked carefully by the S.V. headquarters' staff.

In another space one finds full explanations of abbreviations, including twenty very precise abbreviations concerning colour and markings, and we follow here with the principal ones. If the colour is noted 'sg', this stands for 'schwarz und gelb' (black/tan), 'sgA' stands for 'schwarz mit gelben Abzeichen' (black with tan markings), 'sgrg' stands for 'schwarz-grau mit gelb' (black and grey with tan), while 'sggr' stands for 'schwarz-gelb mit grau' (black/tan with grey). Then we may find 'sgrL', standing for 'schwarz mit grauen Läufen' (black with grey legs). Another combination we find is 'sbAM', for 'schwarz mit braunen Abzeichen und Maske' (black with brown markings and muzzle). The predominant colour is always listed first; so we find 'grg' for 'grau mit gelb' (grey with tan) and 'ggr' for 'gelb mit grau' (tan with grey). The whole range of colours is described in fullest detail. One of the reasons why a dog's pedigree is not stamped for his lifetime until he is eighteen months old is the possibility of a change of colour or markings – something which happens quite frequently. We have ourselves seen sables turn into black/tans, and black dogs turn a light golden sable. In compiling a descriptive report on the dog's ancestors the markings are most essential, and the whole system is extremely well thought out.

Following on you will find long and complicated explanations of the numerous training qualifications, some of which were noted at the beginning of this chapter. The top grading 'V/A' (Vorzüglich-Auslese) is awarded only to a very small group of near-perfect animals – perhaps about a dozen of each sex, and sometimes only half that number – at the annual Hauptzuchtschau, the great national breed show, where there may be between 200 and 300 entries in each Open class. It is, therefore, the crown of the breed; the dog has to be not only practically fault-free but to have the best and most harmonious blood-lines behind it, combined with 100 per cent Shepherd character.

If the pedigree is stamped 'Leistungsheit', it means that both parents and all four grandparents of the dog have won training degrees. This kind of breeding is very much sought after by overseas buyers, and when it is linked with a top breed winner it gives one a complete German Shepherd Dog.

We feel it may be useful to give a glossary of the words and their abbreviations that are most likely to be found in pedigrees, show reports and the like, to be followed by a similar list of the symbols for working qualifications.

Abzeichen (A)	Markings
Ahnen	Ancestors
Ahnentafel	Pedigree
Allgemeine Erscheinung	General appearance
Alter	Age
Alterklasse (AK)	Adult class
Angekört	Examined at breed survey
Augen	Eyes
Ausdruck	Expression
Ausreichend	Satisfactory
Bauch	Belly
Befriedigend (B)	Fair
Behaarung	Coat
Belegt	Bred
Besitzer	Owner
Bewertung	Qualification
Blau	Blue
Braun (br)	Brown
Breit	Broad

Brust (Br)	Breast, chest
Deckfarbe	Predominant colour
Drahthaarig	Wire-coated
Dunkel (d)	Dark
Ehrenpreis	Prize of Honour
Eltern	Parents
Eng	Narrow
Enkel, Enkelin	Grandson, granddaughter
Erziehung	Upbringing, training
Fang	Foreface, muzzle
Farbe	Colour
Fassbeine	Bowlegged
Fassrippe	Barrel-ribbed
Flanke	Loin
Flüchtig	Fleet(ing)
Gang	Gait
Gelb (g)	Gold, tan
Gelbgrau (ggr)	Tan/grey sable
Geschlechtsgepräge	Sex-quality
Gesundheit	Sound health
Gewinkelt	Angulated
Gewolkt	Dingy, mixed colours
Geworfen	Whelped
Glatthaarig	Smooth-coated
Graugelb (grg)	Greyish tan (sable)
Gross	Large
Grosseltern	Grandparents
Gut (G)	Good
Sehr gut (SG)	Very good
Guter Zustand	Fine condition
Hacken	Hocks
Hals	Throat, neck
Harmonisch	Co-ordinated
Hart	Hard
Hasenpfote	Harefoot(ed)
Hell	Light-coloured
Hinterbeine	Hind legs
Hoden	Testicles
Höhe	Height
Hund	Dog
Hündin	Bitch
Jugend	Youth
Jugendklasse (JKL)	Youth class
Junghund	Dog under two years old

Katzenpfote	Catfoot(ed)
Klein	Small
Knocken	Bones
Körbuch	Register of breed surveyed dogs
Körzucht	Good reproductive qualities
Kruppe	Croup
Kurz	Short
Lang	Long
Länge	Length
Langhaarig	Long-coated
Läufe	Legs
Mangelhaft	Faulty
Maske (M)	Mask
Muskeln	Muscles
Mutter	Dam
Nachschub	Drive, thrust
Nagel	Claw
Nase	Nose
Oberarm	Upper arm
Ohren	Ears
Pfote	Paw
Rasse	Breed
Rein	Pure
Rippen	Ribs
Rot (r)	Red
Rude (R)	Dog (male as distinct from female)
Sattel (S)	Saddle
Schädel	Skull
Scheu	Shy
Schulter	Shoulder
Schulterblatt	Shoulderblade
Schussfest	Gun-proof
Schussgleichgültig	Gun-shy
Schwämmig	Spongy, flabby
Schwanz	Tail
Schwarz (s)	Black
Schwarzgelb (sg)	Black/gold, black/tan
Schwarzgrau (sgr)	Black/grey
Silbergrau	Silver/grey
Steil	Steep
Stockhaar	Normal coat
Tief	Deep
Traben	Trot, trotting

German	English
Trocken	Dry
Überbeiss	Overshot
Überwinkelt	Over-angulated
Ungenügend (O) or Null	Unsatisfactory
Vater	Sire
Verein	Club
Verkäuflich (Verk)	For sale
Vorbeiss	Undershot
Vorderbeine	Forelegs
Vorderbrust	Forechest
Vorschub	Reach (of gait)
Vorzüglich	Excellent
Welpe	Puppy
Weich	Soft
Weiches Ohr	Soft-eared
Werfen	To whelp, whelped
Wesen	Temperament
Wesenfest	Firm temperament
Wesenscheu	Shyness
Wetterfest	Weatherproof
Widerrist	Withers
Zotthaarig	Open-coated
Zuchtbuch	Stud book
Zuchtbuchnummer	Stud book number
Zuchter	Breeder
Zuchtprüfung	Approved (approval) as suitable for breeding

There have been a number of changes in recent years in the requirements for the various working degrees. In consequence, it has been thought proper in some cases to change the title of a degree to reflect its changed character and, perhaps, its increased scope. For in many cases, as the versatility of our breed has become more generally appreciated, so the training programme has been enlarged, and some older qualification of strictly limited scope has simply been swallowed up in one of broader character and has become redundant. Here are the current training degrees and their symbols:

Symbol	German	English
AD	Ausdauer	Passed endurance test
BPDH I, II	Bahnpolizeidiensthund	Railway police dog
BlH	Blindenführhund	Guide dog for the blind

DH	Diensthund	Working dog in a service
DPH	Dienstpolizeihund	Service police dog
FH	Fahrtenhund	Tracking dog
HGH	Herdengebrauchshund	Herding dog
Int. Pr. Kl.	Internationale Prüfungsklasse	International trials class
MH I, II	Meldehund	Messenger dog
PFP I, II	Polizeifahrtenhundprüfung	Police tracking-dog test
PH	Polizeihund	Police dog
PSP I, II	Polizeischutzhundprüfung	Police guard dog test
SH I, II	Sanitätshund	Red cross dog
SchH I, II, III	Schutzhund	Guard or defence dog
ZH I, II	Zollhund	Customs dog
ZFH	Zollfahrtenhund	Customs tracker dog
ZPr.	Zuchtprüfung bestanden	Passed temperament test for breeding

As mentioned earlier, an 'x' before a dog's name in a show catalogue denotes that he is angekört – has been examined (and reported on) at a breed survey, but in very old, extended pedigrees, one may still chance upon references to degrees which, as explained above, have now disappeared. The principal ones were these:

BDH	Bahndiensthund	Railway service dog
Kr.H	Kriegshund	War dog
K.SchH	Kriegschutzhund	War defence dog or war guard dog
LS	Leistungsieger	Field trial champion
PDH	Polizeidiensthund	Police dog on patrol service
SuchH	Suchhund	Tracking dog

21   About the Lighter Side
of German Shepherds

We have laid so much emphasis on the serious side of the training, breeding and health aspects of our breed that we feel that the reader may have the impression that we cannot get any fun or enjoyment from owning a German Shepherd Dog – which is very far from the truth. We have gathered together a few anecdotes and news clippings in our time which, together with some of our own experiences, would fill another book on what it means to own a Shepherd Dog! A few of these, with some pictures, would show you how owners enjoy their dogs, and we wish you all the same deep satisfaction and joy from your own dog.

Puppies are always fun, and watching their antics is everyone's favourite way of wasting time. It is extraordinary how a small creature of five or six weeks old can possess a personality, an intelligence and a

This Shepherd Dog is the guardian of a large estate and spends much of his time overlooking his territory from this convenient, if rather strange, vantage point.

This year old dog waits with remarkable patience for his birthday cake share-out.

determination which can distinguish it from its litter-mates, and give you problems before it even leaves the nest. We once had a litter of eight, but when they were let out at ten pm for their supper and a run-round while their bedding was cleaned, only seven could be counted at shutting-up time. A quick torchlight hunt round the run and the missing boy came from nowhere, was received with open arms, petted and spoiled, and went happily to bed. Well, you may have guessed by now that this performance was repeated every night afterwards, the 'laddie baby' going A.W.O.L. until the rest of the litter was in bed, when he appeared like magic for his own special good-night kiss!

Bitches and puppies together are also charming, and the mother instinct, once aroused in a bitch, seems to extend to most small things. Marynka lives on a farm where the cat has her frequent families in the spaces in between the stacked-up hay bales. So each day she visits the cat, stretching in a long leg to paw her out from the hay. The cat then departs to hunt for her dinner, and Marynka wriggles in *backwards* to keep the kittens warm until the cat returns, to put *her* long paw in to fetch Marynka out. On another farm, Gera had the self-appointed task of licking the Siamese cats dry in front of the kitchen range after their hunting expeditions. When she had puppies and was confined to a loose-box, the Siamese used to bring her baby rabbits and drop them in the whelping box – an example of animal understanding seldom seen.

Dogs are very quick to associate smells with occasions of special importance or with favourite people. Our own dogs get gingerbread for their birthday cakes. When it is baking, the word is passed round and everyone tries to rush the kitchen door, expecting the afternoon share-out. They do not react to non-ginger cake baking.

Our dogs make excellent collectors for charities. One of them went recently on a charity walk, inviting sponsorships of 5p per foot per mile, which brought him a fourfold reward. Others collect for the Guide Dogs, and few people can resist the outstretched paw which thanks the donors. How they enjoy these occasions and their particular importance that day, and how we, too, enjoy the praise and recognition they earn so happily.

Trained dogs will enter into all kinds of games with great delight, hide-and-seek being a favourite. This game was turned to quite a different use by an owner when she saw a man walking round the house 'trying' the french windows. On seeing this lady through a window he demanded to be let in – 'or he would break the glass and force an entrance'. Calling quietly to her dog to 'go and hide' the lady then opened a door with a loud command to 'seek!', which the Shepherd Dog did so efficiently that he cornered the startled intruder while his owner rang the police.

The owner of a riding school uses his Shepherd as a messenger between the school and his home. His wife opens the small capsule attached to the collar and reads the slip of paper enclosed, which may say anything from '½-hour late for lunch', to 'Put £1 on Ritzi Mitzi 3.30'.

Dogs can put one in embarrassing situations, too, which may be fun for everyone save the victim, usually oneself. One very cold day I was crossing the farmyard nearby with two adults on leads and one free, plus a refractory five-months puppy, also on the lead. The puppy wound his lead round my legs and so intent was I on unwinding him that I didn't notice a rabbit that had been driven in by the cold to find breakfast in the yard. The dogs saw him, though, and shot off at top speed. The puppy's lead, meanwhile, had latched itself in the edging of my scarlet 'long johns', and so, flat on my back, on the frozen puddles, I was towed along, with a lead attached to my vital winter protection. The lead finally won, and off went the puppy with a large piece of material attached, of the same colour as my face as we came to a halt in front of the farmworkers' breakfast party in an open barn!

There are countless stories of police dogs' bravery and courage and just as many simple home-life anecdotes, such as we have written here,

Baby Sitter Saxon

Above left: Baby watched over by Saxon: 'Just sit quietly there until Mummy comes back, my boy!'

Below left: Baby is thinking of crawling away: 'Now, you're not going off anywhere, my lad!'

Above right: Baby hoists himself up on Saxon's neck to look around for mischief. 'All right, just hold onto my neck, but stay close.'

Below right: Baby is rescued at the water's edge as frantic mother arrives: 'Ah! Just reached you in time, Mummy's close behind.'

Saxon has heart-to-heart talk with baby about the dangers of wandering away: 'Now look here, old chap, you simply must *not* play near the water, understand!'

which show how our dog can enter into our lives and share most of the things we do. And it is only when living like this that his full potential is realized, and we see our dog in his true light – as centuries of serving mankind have made him, the finest four-footed companion of all, the splendid partner of equally splendid men in our police forces.

With this tribute we end this book, always humble in our service to the breed we hold in the greatest affection, and ever grateful for the devotion they have returned a hundredfold – devotion which has made life's bright patches brighter, and has helped us through the days when we did not feel like laughing.

Appendix: Addresses

Some Useful Addresses For Breed and Training Enquiries

ASSOCIATED SHEEP, POLICE AND ARMY DOGS SOCIETY
President: Mrs C. N. Fleet, 95 Cornwall Road, Ruislip Manor, Middlesex.

GERMAN SHEPHERD DOG LEAGUE OF GREAT BRITAIN
Secretary: Mrs J. Ixer, Silver Lee, Sparsholt, Winchester, Hants, SO21 2NZ. Tel. 096 272 239

BRITISH ASSOCIATION FOR GERMAN SHEPHERD DOGS
Secretary: Miss M. M. Webb, 55a South Road, Erdington, Birmingham 23. Tel. 021 373 3424

ALSATIAN CLUB OF SCOTLAND
Secretary: Mrs A. Adam, Mosslea Kennels, Longriggend, nr Airdrie, Lanarks.

MIDLAND COUNTIES GERMAN SHEPHERD DOG ASSOCIATION
Secretary: Mrs J. Haywood, Ashlands, 47 Buttery Lane, Skegby, Sutton-in-Ashfield, Nottinghamshire. Tel. Sutton-in-Ashfield 2898

GERMAN SHEPHERD CLUB OF NORTHERN IRELAND
Secretary: Mrs H. L. McCune, 143 Greyabbey Raod, Ballywalter, Co. Down, N. Ireland.

GERMAN SHEPHERD CLUB OF IRELAND
Secretary: Mr S. Styles, 97 Elm Mount Avenue, Beaumont, Dublin, Eire.

THE KENNEL CLUB
1 Clarges Street, Piccadilly, London W1Y 8AB.

Suppliers of Food and Diet Supplements

C. F. ABEL, Forest Road, Charlbury, Oxfordshire.
Bone meal tablets with Vitamin D (instead of calcium), seaweed tablets, chlorophyll tablets (protection for bitches), etc.

DENES VETERINARY HEALTH PRODUCTS LTD, 14 Goldstone Street, Hove, East Sussex, BN3 3RL.
Gastric tablets (helpful for minor stomach upsets and teething), greenleaf tablets, garlic tablets, seaweed powder and tablets.

Breed Standard

GENERAL APPEARANCE Slightly long in comparison to height; of powerful, well-muscled build with weather-resistant coat. Relation between height, length, position and structure of fore and hindquarters (angulation) producing far-reaching, enduring gait. Clear definition of masculinity and femininity essential, and working ability never sacrificed for mere beauty.

CHARACTERISTICS Versatile working dog, balanced and free from exaggeration. Attentive, alert, resilient and tireless with keen scenting ability.

TEMPERAMENT Steady of nerve, loyal, self-assured, courageous and tractable. Never nervous, over-aggressive or shy.

HEAD & SKULL Proportionate in size to body, never coarse, too fine or long. Clean cut; fairly broad between ears. Forehead slightly domed; little or no trace of central furrow. Cheeks forming softly rounded curve, never protruding. Skull from ears to bridge of nose tapering gradually and evenly, blending without too pronounced stop into wedge shaped powerful muzzle. Skull approximately 50% of overall length of head. Width of skull corresponding approximately to length, in males slightly greater, in females slightly less. Muzzle strong, lips firm, clean and closing tightly. Top of muzzle straight, almost parallel to forehead. Short, blunt, weak, pointed, overlong muzzle undesirable.

EYES Medium sized, almond-shaped, never protruding. Dark brown preferred, lighter shade permissible, provided expression good and general harmony of head not destroyed. Expression lively, intelligent and self-assured.

EARS Medium sized, firm in texture, broad at base, set high, carried erect, almost parallel, never pulled inwards or tipped, tapering to a point, open at front. Never hanging. Folding back during movement permissible.

MOUTH Jaws strongly developed. With a perfect, regular and complete scissor bite, i.e. upper teeth closely overlapping lower teeth and set square to the jaw. Teeth healthy and strong. Full dentition desirable.

NECK Fairly long, strong, with well developed muscles, free from throatiness. Carried at 45 degrees angle to horizontal, raised when excited, lowered at fast trot.

FOREQUARTERS Shoulder blades long, set obliquely (45 degrees) laid flat to body. Upper arm strong, well muscled, joining shoulder blade at approximately 90 degrees. Forelegs straight from pasterns to elbows viewed from any angle, bone oval rather than round. Pasterns firm, supple and slightly angulated. Elbows neither tucked in nor turned out. Length of foreleg exceeding depth of chest.

BODY Length measured from point of breast bone to rear of pelvis, exceeding height at withers. Correct ratio 10 to 9 or 8 and a half. Under-sized dogs, stunted growth, high-legged dogs, those too heavy or too light in build, over-loaded fronts, too short overall appearance, any feature detracting from reach or endurance of gait, undesirable. Chest deep (45%–48%) of height at shoulder, not too broad, brisket long, well developed. Ribs well formed and long; neither barrel-shaped not too flat; allowing free movement of elbows when gaiting. Relatively short loin. Belly firm, only slightly drawn up. Back between withers and croup, straight, strongly developed, not too long. Overall length achieved by correct angle of well laid shoulders, correct length of croup and hindquarters. Withers long, of good height and well defined, joined back in smooth line without disrupting flowing top-line, slightly sloping from front to back. Weak, soft and roach backs undesirable and should be rejected. Loin broad, strong, well muscled. Croup long, gently curving downwards to tail without disrupting flowing top-line. Short, steep or flat croups undesirable.

HINDQUARTERS Overall strong, broad and well-muscled, enabling effortless forward propulsion of whole body. Upper thighbone, viewed from side, sloping to slightly longer lower thighbone. Hind angulation sufficient if imaginary line dropped from point of buttocks cuts through lower thigh just in front of hock, continuing down slightly in front of hind feet. Angulations corresponding approximately with front angulation, without over-angulation, hock strong. Any tendency towards over-angulation of hindquarters reduces firmness and endurance.

FEET Rounded toes well-closed and arched. Pads well-cushioned and durable. Nails short, strong and dark in colour. Dewclaws removed from hindlegs.

TAIL Bushy-haired, reaches at least to hock—ideal length reaching to middle of metatarsus. At rest tail hangs in slight sabre-like curve; when moving raised and curve increased, ideally never above level of back. Short, rolled, curled, generally carried badly or stumpy from birth, undesirable.

GAIT/MOVEMENT Sequence of step follows diagonal pattern, moving foreleg and opposite hindleg forward simultaneously; hind foot thrust forward to midpoint of body and having equally long reach with forefeet without any noticeable change in backline.

COAT Outer coat consisting of straight, hard, close lying hair as dense as possible; thick undercoat. Hair on head, ears front of legs, paws and toes short; on back, longer and thicker; in some males forming slight ruff. Hair longer on back of legs as far down as pasterns and stifles and forming fairly thick trousers on hindquarters. No hard and fast rule for length of hair; mole-type coats undesirable.

COLOUR Black or black saddle with tan, or gold to light grey markings. All black, all grey, or grey with lighter or brown markings referred to as Sables. Nose black. Light markings on chest or very pale colour on inside of legs permissible but undesirable, as are whitish nails, red tipped tails or wish-washy faded colours defined as lacking in pigmentation. Blues, livers, albinos, whites (i.e. almost pure white dogs with black noses) and near white *highly undesirable*. Undercoat, except in all black dogs, usually grey or fawn. Colour in itself is of secondary importance having no effect on character or fitness for work. Final colour of a young dog only ascertained when outer coat has developed.

SIZE Ideal height (from withers and just touching elbows): Dogs 62.5 cm (25 ins). Bitches 57.5 cm (23 ins). 2.5 cm (1 in) either above or below ideal permissible.

FAULTS Any departure from the foregoing points should be considered a fault and the seriousness with which the fault should be regarded should be in exact proportion to its degree.

NOTE Male animals should have two apparently normal testicles fully descended into the scrotum.

© The Kennel Club 1986

Index

Names of dogs are indicated by quotation marks